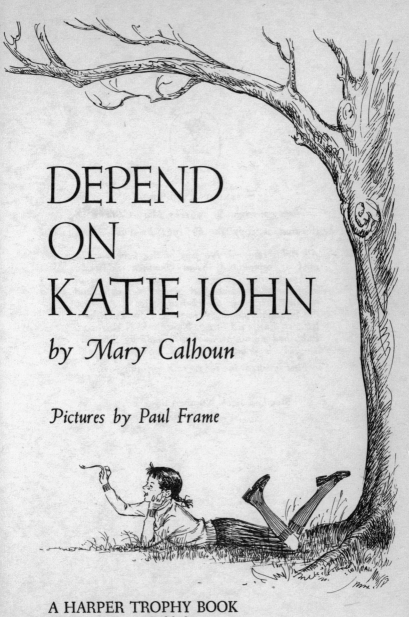

DEPEND ON KATIE JOHN

by Mary Calhoun

Pictures by Paul Frame

A HARPER TROPHY BOOK
Harper & Row, Publishers
New York, Evanston, San Francisco, London

Contents

Also by Mary Calhoun

KATIE JOHN

HONESTLY, KATIE JOHN!

DEPEND
ON
KATIE JOHN

Katie John, Landlady

Katie John stopped short as she passed the mirror. Goodness, was that a wrinkle on her forehead? Wrinkles already, at the age of almost-eleven? She leaned forward with her arms full of curtains. No, it was only a wavy spot in the aged mirror. Katie John smiled at herself in the mirror, then made a face to show she wasn't admiring herself, then worked a hand loose from the curtains to pat down her spiky bangs.

It was a wonder she wasn't getting wrinkles, with all the worry and flurry of getting ready for renters. When she and her parents had decided to rent out rooms, Katie John had thought all their problems were solved. Ha!

She carried the curtains to the hall, dropped them over the banister, and watched them float down the stair well to the first-floor hall. She loved looking down from the third floor like this, looking down through the heart of the house. Good old house. From here she could see just the front of the wide second-floor hallway, with Mother's red geraniums on the chest under the windows. Below her the banisters gleamed from the pol-

3

ishing Katie had given them, sliding down them so much last summer. Lately, though, she'd decided that she was getting too old for such nonsense. At the bottom of the stair well was the faded green hall rug that ran back to the kitchen. She could see the hatrack, too, with its moose head at the top. Next to it stood a little marble-topped table on which Mother always kept a bowl of flowers, a pink potted begonia now that it was winter. Beyond, Katie John could see a glimpse of the heavy front door with its frosty etched panes, the door through which family and friends had passed for over ninety years.

As Katie John went back for more curtains she shook her head at how silly and young she'd been when she'd first come here with her parents early last summer. Then she'd hated the old brick house because it seemed square and ugly, and because she missed California, and because she thought Barton's Bluff was a poky little town, stuck back here in the Missouri woods by the Mississippi River. Way back then she could hardly wait for her folks to sell the house Mother's Aunt Emily had left when she died.

By November, though, Katie John loved the house so much she couldn't bear to leave it. Mother and Dad felt the same way, and it was then that they decided to rent out rooms.

"Not that I want to share the house my great-grand-father built with a whole bunch of people," Katie said firmly to the wavy mirror as she passed it, "but it's a Problem of Money."

Dad had quit his newspaper job in California to write a book. At first they'd planned to live in New York City on the money they got from selling the house. But Dad still hadn't finished his book, and if they didn't sell the house, then money had to come from somewhere. So they'd decided to rent out most of the twenty rooms and live on that money.

Katie John had wanted to stay in the old house so badly that she'd even promised to help Mother with all the work of caring for the renters. There certainly had been work enough, just getting ready for them. All the rooms had to be cleaned, some of the furniture had to be mended and polished. And there had been a wild week when she and her parents had tried to paint some of the high-ceilinged rooms. Katie sighed as she remembered all the paint she'd spilled that week.

She dropped another armload of curtains down the stair well. This was one of her bright ideas to save steps. It was lots easier and more fun to watch the curtains float down than to march up and down two flights of stairs carrying curtains. Drat. One of the curtains was caught on the second-floor banister. At the last minute Mother had decided to wash all the third-floor curtains again, so they'd be crisp when People started coming to look at the rooms.

Only, where were all the people? That was another

worry. The "Rooms for Rent" ad had been in the newspaper for a week now, and nobody had come. What if no one rented the rooms, after all this work?

Katie John stood on a window seat and slid another curtain off its rod. Of course, they had two renters already: Miss Howell and her sister, Miss Julia. Miss Howell was Katie's fifth-grade teacher, and she and her sister moved to town from their farm every winter. Katie had been so proud of herself when she'd persuaded Miss Howell to rent two rooms and a bath on the second floor.

However, it had taken all of Miss Howell's first month's rent money to fix up the rest of the house for renters. It seemed as if Katie and her folks had been living on hamburger and beans for weeks now. They just had to have more renters paying money soon.

Katie John tossed the curtains over the banisters— oh, dear! Someone was in the hall below! She grabbed at the air, but it was too late. "Look out!" she cried, as the curtains flew down the stair well toward the tall woman with the piled-up white hair. The woman looked up just as the curtains descended over her face and shoulders like a veil. The woman stood frozen under her draperies. Katie gave a squeak, half-gasp, half-giggle.

Mother was down there, too, her upturned face horrified. "Katie John Tucker!" And to the woman, "Oh, I'm so sorry!" as she tried to untangle the curtains.

Katie ran down the two flights of stairs. She hoped the woman hadn't wanted to—it would be just her luck

—yes, the woman was saying through her veilings, "wanted to rent a room, but—"

Oh, dear!

The lace curtains were caught on the lady's hairpins. Mother was trying to work the cloth loose without disturbing the handsome high hair-do. Katie reached to help, but Mother stopped her with a look.

"—would never do!" the lady was saying, throwing the curtains back from her face. "I must live in a house with some dignity to it. I try to live graciously!"

She tore the curtains from her head. The lace ripped, hairpins flew, and her hair toppled.

"Yes, I understand," Mother murmured, picking up hairpins.

"Never do!" the woman declared, gathering her hair into a knot and jabbing in pins. "Never do!" She swept out of the house.

Silently Katie John and her mother watched the no-longer prospective renter march down the front walk and away. At last Katie looked at Mother.

"I guess I've done it again," she said. "Depend on me to mess things up."

Mother sighed, then smiled at Katie. "Maybe she wouldn't have made a good renter, anyway. She seemed pretty crusty."

Katie shook her head. "We can't afford to be choosey. I'm sorry, Mother, really."

"I know, honey." Mother gave Katie's shoulders a quick squeeze.

Katie John gathered up the curtains from the floor, giving Mother the torn ones. The rest she carried down to the basement laundry room. It was all very well to say she was sorry, easy to say it. But when you're sorry, you should do something to show it, Katie thought. I could wash the curtains for Mother.

But that wouldn't bring the lady renter back. No, the best thing she could do would be to find another renter. How?

"Katie," Mother called down the cellar stairs, "will you go to the fish market for me?"

Promptly Katie John dropped the curtains and headed for the stairs, relieved she could do something for Mother besides washing all those curtains. She felt a little guilty, though, now that she wasn't really making a sacrifice. Who wouldn't rather go jaunting off to the fish market at the river than spend the morning alone in the basement washing curtains? Katie John got the secret shudders when she thought of all the housework in the months ahead, helping Mother keep this big house clean for renters. But Mother couldn't do it without help, and Katie had insisted that Mother could depend on her, if only they could continue to live in the house.

Katie got the fish money and her coat. Outside, she eyed the heavy gray sky and hoped those clouds held snow. Here it was almost Christmas, and no snow yet. She'd seen snow in California, of course, twice when they'd driven up to the mountains. But she'd never seen snow falling right outside the windows of her own house, or had it handy on her front lawn.

Down the block she stopped at Sue Halsey's house. Sue was her age and her best friend in Barton's Bluff. The sound of piano playing stopped when she rang the doorbell, and Sue came to the door.

"Hey, come on," Katie urged. "We're going to the river! To the fish market!"

"Oh, Katie." Sue laughed. "You make it sound as if we were going to see the queen. All right, as soon as I finish practicing."

Katie John sat down to wait. Sue was so good. She was always ready to go wherever Katie suggested. Sometimes she suspected Sue went along to get her out of trouble. Which was silly, of course, because Sue was the one who got the most flustered. Anyway, there wasn't going to be any trouble today—any more trouble, she corrected herself.

She watched Sue's plump hands move smoothly over the keys, picking out a minuet. Sue hit a wrong note, hit it again, then went over and over that passage until she had it worked out. There was a piano at Katie's house, too, but no money for piano lessons yet. Katie wasn't too sorry. She'd never have Sue's patience.

"There," Sue said. "Let's go."

"We almost had a renter," Katie John said on the way out. She told Sue what had happened and declared, "I've just got to find another renter to take that lady's place. Are any of your relatives moving to town for the winter?"

Sue had many aunts and uncles and cousins, both in Barton's Bluff and in the countryside around. But none of them planned to move, she said.

Then who? You couldn't go up to people on the street and ask them if they wanted to rent a room. It wasn't dignified, Katie said, remembering the tall woman.

"It should be someone nice and quiet and dignified," she decided.

"Well, the nicest people in town go to the public library," Sue said. "Maybe we—"

"Sue, that's a wonderful idea!" Katie whirled to grab Sue's shoulders. "We could ask Miss Squires and the other librarians if they want to rent a room, or if they know anyone who does. And we could ask people as they come in the library. It isn't as if they'd be strangers."

What a nice houseful they'd have. A teacher and her gentle sister, people who loved to read books, maybe a librarian, too. Katie John felt as good as if she already had a renter. They'd go to the library just as soon as they got the fish.

"Come on!"

She ran down the steps in the sidewalk of the steep

hill that dropped to the river, skipping every other step. Sue hurried after her, one step at a time. Below, the Mississippi spread wide and dark under the December sky, with white sandy beaches and wooded hills on the opposite side. The water looked almost black, edged with little white ruffles of waves whipped by the wind. Out from the shore a towboat and its long finger of barges was passing slowly downstream. Someone was rowing a boat out to the tow, or maybe it was just a fisherman. Several fishermen's rowboats dotted the river.

Katie liked to watch the towboats going on down the river, around the bend, beyond these hills to somewhere far.

"Maybe they're going clear to New Orleans," she said. "Do you suppose the men have to take summer clothes, too, for the warm weather down south?"

Sue shivered. "I don't see how it could be summery in New Orleans when it's so cold here. Anyway, we won't be seeing the boats much longer this winter."

"Why not?"

Because the river here above St. Louis was just about closed in the winter, Sue explained. The boats couldn't travel easily because of the ice. By next month the ice would extend from the shore far out into the river. Along the shore the ice was often thick enough to walk on, she added.

"You mean we can hike on the Mississippi River?" Katie made a mental note to remember that.

"Well, it isn't safe to go very far out," Sue said, beginning to look worried.

"Oh, never mind, Sue. Let's buy the fish and get up to the library."

Katie John hurried toward the shack on the riverbank. It smelled fishy down here, but fishy in a clean, pleasant way, with a brisk breeze mixing in the coolness of the river. A splintering wooden dock ran from the fish market out over the water, and several rowboats were tied to the dock pilings. A small boy was playing at the end of the dock, and a man was just coming up from his boat with a string of fish. Anyone could sell whatever he caught to the fish market. Customers never knew what kind of fish the market would have, or if there'd be any fish at all.

Katie John started to go in the door, then stopped. Now the dock was empty. What had become of the little boy? My goodness—surely he hadn't— She ran out on the dock. Heavens, yes. He'd fallen in! He'd drown!

Katie barely knew how to swim, but she flung away her coat and plunged off the dock. Oh! Oh! The water was so cold! So *wet,* when the last thing you expected five minutes ago was to be wet clear to your skin. She thrashed with her arms to pull her head up out of the water. The little boy was splashing a few feet away.

"D-don't wo-wor-r-ry," Katie chattered. "I'll g-get you."

She kicked, and a heavy pain gripped her leg. It

dragged her down in the icy water. Katie spluttered up again, shouting "Help!"

Next thing a wiry arm grabbed her head and towed her to the dock. The arm belonged to the little boy.

"Here, get up." He pushed her toward the ladder.

Sue was jumping up and down, screaming, and men were running out from the fish market. Safe on the dock, Katie John turned on the boy, who'd scrambled up the ladder behind her.

"I thought you were drowning," she accused.

The boy looked down at the puddle of water running from him, shrugged his shoulders, and grinned.

"You kids get in out of the cold."

One of the men hustled the children into the fish market. Sue followed with Katie's coat, while Katie John shivered, partly from the cold, partly from the embarrassment of it all. Saved by the child she'd tried to rescue!

Inside the shack a short, skinny man knelt down and opened a suitcase. He took out some clothes and handed them to the boy.

"Here, son, go change," he said patiently. To the girls he added, "I always carry a change of clothes for Buster. He falls in the water pert near every time he gets close to it. That boy don't need saving. Swims like a fish."

"That's n-nice," Katie chattered bitterly. "P-please thank him for s-saving me." She turned to take her coat from Sue.

"Here, you can't go out wet like that," the man said.

He dug in his suitcase, pulled out a shirt and pants that must have been his. Over Katie's protests he made her go behind the fish counter and change into those clothes. It was decided that the man would walk home with Katie and Sue so he could get his clothes back. Katie rolled the baggy pants legs up and pulled on her coat as Buster emerged from the back of the market. He grinned silently at Katie and headed for the dock again, but his father caught him by the ear. The fish-market man wrapped Katie's wet clothes in a newspaper, and they all started up the hill.

"Name's Peters," the man said. "Riverman. We just come offa that tow." He nodded to the towboat disappearing down the river.

Mr. Peters hardly appeared big enough for the heavy work on the barges, but his face was tan and wind-roughed. He had a round little nose and round brown button eyes that made him look cheery. Like a gingerbread man, Katie thought, if a gingerbread man had worked out in the wind and sun on the river.

"Yeah!" Buster spoke suddenly. "Some towboat!"

"Does Buster go on the boat with you all the time?" Katie asked. She shifted her bundle of clothing. Her wet things were soaking through the newspaper.

"No, I just picked Buster up yesterday."

The little riverman explained that Buster stayed with his aunt in Iowa while his father was working on the river. The winters, when the river season was closed, he spent with his father. Buster was in the second grade, Mr. Peters added proudly.

Katie didn't think that was anything to be so proud of. Everyone went through second grade sooner or later. She looked at Buster. Just as his father hardly looked big enough for river work, so Buster hardly looked big enough for second grade. He had a round head like his father's, with pale brown hair as short and smooth as mouse fur. He had a button nose, too, but Katie couldn't see his eyes because he kept them down.

"Fish-market man didn't know of any rooms for rent," Mr. Peters was saying to Buster. "We'll try uptown after we deliver these little ladies."

Katie John stopped short, clutching her wet bundle to her chest.

"Did you say 'rooms for rent'?" she demanded. "Are you looking for a room?"

"Well, yes," said Mr. Peters. "We figured we'd winter here where I can work at the flour mill."

"I'll rent you a room!" Katie exclaimed. "We've got all kinds of rooms for rent. Right up there." She pointed to the red-brick house at the top of the hill.

"Well, now," Mr. Peters said cautiously, "I was sort of hoping to rent a room where the landlady would keep an eye on Buster after school."

Katie John thought fast. Mother wouldn't have time to do that, with all the rest of the work. Dad mustn't be bothered if he was ever going to finish writing his book. And the last thing Katie wanted was some little water-crazy kid tagging around after her. Still, she just had to find a renter somewhere, and here were two of them, dumped right in her lap. Besides, the boy had saved her life, Katie thought sourly. She supposed she owed him something.

"I could look after Buster," Katie John told Mr. Peters. "We've got a nice big yard that he could play in, a whole half of a block, really. And our rooms are awfully nice."

"Well, then, that's just fine," Mr. Peters said, his button eyes bright. "Buster and me, we'll just take a look at your rooms."

Buster walked up on Katie John's heels, but when she turned he grinned as if to apologize and looked down again. Katie looked at him sharply. This little boy was too quiet. But his eyes weren't. Now she'd had a glimpse of them, and there was a devilish look flecked in Buster's eyes. Katie wondered what she was getting into. Then, as they approached her front gate, she thought of something else.

Oh, dear. Oh, well.

Katie John ran ahead into the house.

"Mother," she called, "I forgot the fish, but I found a renter!"

Her father was standing in the front hall. He looked at his daughter, dressed in men's clothing, carrying a wet bundle and followed by a strange man, a strange boy, and Sue. He looked at her happy face and shook his head, laughing.

"Depend on Katie John!" he said.

Cousin Ben

As Katie John pinned the sheets on the line her mind hummed along happily, as if she were purring silently inside. Some days she felt all torn up and mad or discontented, and those days she said she felt grubbly. But today was a happy hum day. Everything was going along just right. The house was filling up with renters, the sky was blue and bright, and this afternoon she was going Christmas shopping with Sue.

" 'What is so rare as a day in December, then if ever come perfect days,' " Katie misquoted gaily from a poem the fifth grade had started learning yesterday, " 'then heaven tries earth if it be in tune, and over it softly her warm ear lays.' "

Of course, the poet, Tennyson, had been talking about June, but today was just as in tune, for Katie, anyway, as a day in June.

Katie John liked poetry with a good bounce to it, and she was glad Miss Howell had a poetry-memorizing period every Friday. Miss Howell was another thing she liked about life. Often, of an evening, when Katie carried up the kindling for the Howell sisters' fireplace, she'd sit and chat by the fire with her teacher. They'd talk about books and poetry and grown-up things, while Miss Julia smiled and watered her many house plants.

Gentle Miss Julia had made the apartment a regular greenhouse of ivy on the walls, African violets, and windows full of geraniums. Miss Julia seldom joined the conversations, but one evening when Miss Howell was reading a fairy tale Miss Julia had startled Katie by murmuring that she still thought that someday her prince would come. Now wasn't that sweet? Even an old lady —she must be at least fifty—could be romantic.

" 'The world is so full of a number of things, I'm sure we should all be as happy as kings,' " Katie added, switching to Robert Louis Stevenson.

Another happy thing was that the Tuckers had a new renter. Mr. Peters had sent up from the flour mill a man who was looking for a room. Mother hadn't been home when the heavy-set man, Mr. Watkins, had come, so Katie John had shown him the rooms. It was more fun than playing store. Mr. Watkins had picked one of the small third-floor bedrooms because they were cheaper and because it was quiet and away from things up there. He was the night watchman for the flour mill, so he slept days and worked nights.

Mr. Peters and Buster had settled in the basement apartment. The house was built on a hill so steep that the basement was actually the ground floor in back. The apartment used to be servants' quarters, and it consisted of three rooms and a bathroom. It was just right for the Peters, especially as it opened on the back yard, where Buster could play. Of course, the Peters had been here only a week, but so far Buster hadn't caused Katie much trouble. He and a little boy from across the street had been busy running trucks and digging in an old sand pile in the back yard almost every afternoon.

Buster came out of his door, and Katie John remembered she was supposed to keep track of him this morning. His father worked until noon on Saturdays.

Buster was looking at a crumpled paper in his hand. "One, two, three," he counted, taking three careful steps straight ahead. He turned sharply to the right. "One, two, three, four," he counted, stepping.

"What are you doing?" Katie asked. "What have you got?"

"Treasure map." Buster showed the paper.

"A treasure map!" Katie ran to see.

On the dirty paper was a line of penciled dots that jogged right and left down to the bottom of the page to a big "X."

"Where did you get this?" Katie John demanded. After all her hunting for mysteries and secret passages in the old house, had this little squirt found a treasure map right away?

"Made it," said Buster, with the same economy of words that his father used.

"You—oh, you silly child!" Katie laughed. "How do

you expect to find treasure, when you made the map yourself?"

"Will, though," said Buster. "Gonna dig when I get to the X." He waved a toy shovel in his other hand. "One, two." He set off again, taking a step for each dot.

"You be careful where you dig," Katie called after him. "Don't dig up the lawn."

She wasn't worried. The ground was so hard with frost that he probably couldn't break it with that toy shovel, anyway. Katie watched Buster stepping and turning across the frozen stalks of what had been Great-Aunt Emily's vegetable garden. She laughed and shook her head. Funny little kid. He'd even torn and smudged the paper to make it look old. Actually, making a treasure map sounded sort of like fun—for a little child. Too bad he wouldn't find anything when he got to X. Maybe sometime she'd make a real treasure hunt for him. She could bury a nickel in a box and then make a map with dots that would lead him to the "treasure." Anyway, his treasure map should keep him busy this morning. She wouldn't have to worry about him.

Katie John left the empty laundry basket in the basement and ran upstairs. The doorbell was ringing, and Mother was just going to the front door. Maybe it would be someone else wanting to rent a room. Katie crowded behind Mother to see.

A man with a stringy white beard stood on the front porch, an old-fashioned black valise and a lumpy burlap sack at his feet. His clothes looked as if he'd slept in them, and his chin whiskers could stand a good combing. A twig was caught in them. The man lifted his old hat and showed a shining bald head with just a fringe of speckled gray hair above his ears.

"Howdy do, Cousin Abigail," he said to Mother. "I'm your cousin Ben Orlick from down country. Bet you been fretting why none of the family showed up to welcome you back to Missouri, Abigail. Well, there ain't hardly any family left in these parts. But here's old Cousin Ben to give you all the news of what's left of 'em."

Mother looked puzzled. "Who?" she began, then had to step back, tripping over Katie, because the stranger picked up his valise and sack and walked in. He stared around the front hall.

"Well, well, the old Clark place certain'y has run down," he declared. "Not like the old days. And looky here at this scratch on the banister. Been sliding down it in hobnailed pants, young lady?"

The happy hum in Katie John sputtered. She and her folks had just painted the front hall, and they thought it looked fine. She opened her mouth, but the stranger had gone right on talking.

"Well, sir, I heard tell you folks were living in the old Clark place now, since Emily died, and I just decided I'd come visit you a spell. Things get pretty slow down on the farm, come winter." He moved into the parlor and sat down in the best chair. "I got a big load of firewood in and chopped a mess of kindling, so sister Louisey can get along just dandy without me. Then I says to myself—"

Mother finally interrupted. "Ben Orlick? I'm afraid I don't—"

"Why, sure, you know your cousin Ben Orlick. My Aunt Hallie was your grandma's—"

He began a complicated family history that lost Katie right at the beginning. She watched the twig on his beard bob and waggle, but it wouldn't fall off. The old man ended, "Your daddy and me was second cousins once removed, Cousin Abigail."

The dazed expression on Mother's face faded. Now she simply looked as if she wished it weren't true. It was strange to hear Mother called "Cousin Abigail"; Dad and her friends always called her Abby.

Cousin Ben turned his attention to Katie.

"What's this young'un's name? She your only one?"

Mother nodded and introduced Katie.

"Katie John, hey? Bet you named her after your father, John. Wanted to make sure he was remembered even if you didn't have any sons, hey, Cousin Abigail?" He winked and looked pleased with himself.

Mother didn't. Cousin Ben had guessed right, but after all, Katie's name was their own private business.

"You've come to visit?" Mother began.

"Yes, sir, and I didn't come empty-handed, neither." Cousin Ben rummaged in the burlap sack. "This here gunny sack is plumb full of squash." He pulled out an orange gourd-shaped vegetable. "Makes the best pie in the world. Maybe you'll want to cook up one for supper, Abigail."

"Squash pie!" The corners of Katie's mouth drew down.

"It's like pumpkin pie, honey," Mother murmured, accepting the sack of squash with something less than excitement.

The doorbell shrilled. Katie ran to answer it, and found Buster and an angry-looking little woman on the porch. The woman was Miss Crackenberry from next door, and Katie had discovered long ago that it was the same as having a witch next door. Miss Crackenberry was tiny, hardly taller than Katie, she wore long black skirts, and her nose crooked over just like a witch's nose. She was always cross as a witch, too. Now she was more than cross. She was furious. She had Buster by the ear, and in her other hand were what seemed to be onions with dirt clinging to them.

"No treasure," Buster told Katie John in disgust. "Just onions." His head was cocked sideways, trying to pull his ear loose from the old lady's bony fingers.

"Onions, indeed!" Miss Crackenberry gasped, her face streaked with red splotches. "They're my prize tulip bulbs! Katie, where's your mother?"

She pushed into the house, dragging Buster with her. "This young monster has dug up my prize tulip

bulbs!" she exclaimed to Mrs. Tucker. "Cut some in two! He must be punished! Punished!"

"Oh, dear." Mother's eyes were beginning to look quite wild as she turned from Cousin Ben to Miss Crackenberry. "Katie, why weren't you watching Buster?"

Katie John hunched her shoulders. That's right, Buster was her responsibility.

"I'm terribly sorry, Miss Crackenberry," Katie said. "I'll help you plant the bulbs again. And I'll see that Buster doesn't bother you any more." She shot him a black look. The happy hum had disappeared entirely, and she felt definitely grubbly.

Miss Crackenberry let go of Buster's ear and took notice of the bearded stranger.

"Hello, Ben Orlick," she said dryly. "I see you're back before snow flies."

Cousin Ben nodded to her, also without enthusiasm.

Miss Crackenberry moved back to the hall. She whispered loudly to Mother, "Better get rid of that Ben Orlick right away, or he'll camp on you all winter, same as he did your Aunt Emily. And talk your ear off, to boot."

"Ssh! Ssh!" Mother was afraid Cousin Ben would hear.

"I don't know why Emily Clark put up with him," Miss Crackenberry's whisper hissed just as loud. "He's nothing but a shirt-tail relation!"

She spit out the words as if she'd wadded Cousin Ben

in a little ball and thrown him away. As Katie closed the door after her, she almost felt sorry for Cousin Ben. She didn't like him much herself, but if being against him meant being on Miss Crackenberry's side, she didn't want that, either.

" 'Sat Santy Claus?" Buster whispered suddenly to Katie. He was staring from the hall at Cousin Ben.

"What? No, silly," Katie giggled. "That's our Cousin Ben."

Buster looked unconvinced. "But he got a beard and a sack."

"Well, he isn't Santa Claus. Look, Buster, you stay away from Miss Crackenberry's yard, you hear? Or she's liable to spank you next time."

Buster's eyes were down again. He still had the crumpled treasure map in his hand. Katie John took pity on him and added that later today she'd make a real treasure hunt for him. If it weren't that now she'd have to go help Miss Crackenberry plant her tulip bulbs, she wouldn't be sorry at all that Buster had dug up the old lady's garden. It served her right. Last summer Miss Crackenberry's snappy little dog, Prince, kept digging up Aunt Emily's vegetable garden.

In the parlor Cousin Ben had been telling Mother all about what a trial it had been for Aunt Emily to have to live next door to Miss Crackenberry. Now he was picking up his valise.

"I'll just go up and rest till dinner, Cousin Abigail,"

he said. "All right if I take the front bedroom on the east? That's the one Emily always gave me."

Mother opened her mouth, then shrugged her shoulders as Cousin Ben headed up the stairs. The east bedroom was a big, choice room with a private bathroom and a view of the river. Katie knew Mother had hoped to rent that room for a good price.

"How long do you think he'll visit?" Katie whispered.

"It isn't polite to ask," Mother said. She sighed as she picked up the sack of squash.

As the days passed, Cousin Ben said nothing about leaving. He talked and talked about everything else, until Mother said her ears were ringing and she knew the life history of every family in Ben Orlick's home county. Cousin Ben showed up at the dinner table for every meal. In between meals he talked, occasionally suggesting to Dad ways he could fix up the old house, just as if Dad hadn't been working on repairs for the past month. Dad usually escaped to his bedroom to write, though, so Mother and Katie served as Cousin Ben's audience most often.

Mother had to turn away two ladies who would have liked to rent Cousin Ben's bedroom. At that she hinted to Cousin Ben that the house would be filling up with renters soon, and that the bustle would be disturbing to him. He replied that he liked to see a big houseful over Christmas. Then the Tuckers hoped that he meant to leave after the holidays. After all, it was not unusual for relatives to go visiting at Christmas time. Katie was patient even when Cousin Ben supervised the exact placement of each ornament on the Christmas tree.

Besides, one good thing had come of Cousin Ben's stay, Katie decided. Buster remained convinced that the bearded visitor was Santa Claus, and had been on his best behavior.

But Christmas and New Year's came and passed, and Cousin Ben said not a word about leaving. He seemed settled for the winter in the upstairs bedroom.

At last the Tuckers held council one evening after the old man had gone to bed. They needed rent money coming in on his bedroom, and Cousin Ben showed no signs of paying. In fact, he hadn't contributed a thing to the household since he'd given Mother the sack of squash.

"And I'm so tired of cooking squash." Mother laughed in spite of it all.

"Ugh," Katie John added. The squash hadn't been too bad the first night, but Cousin Ben had urged Mother to cook it almost every day. And squash pie was *not* Katie's idea of pumpkin pie.

Finally Dad slapped his hands on the table. "We'll just have to do it," he said. "Tomorrow I'll tell Ben we need the room for renting purposes. He was a businessman once—ran a store, I believe—and he'll understand how it is with a business."

The Tuckers went to bed relieved. The problem would be solved. They didn't know that the matter had gone out of their hands. An unusually cold mass of air from Canada reached Barton's Bluff about midnight, and the temperature dropped toward zero. At the same time the ancient furnace in the cellar gave up the struggle to keep twenty rooms warm in that kind of weather.

Katie John roused in her little room off the kitchen and reached for another blanket, only to find that all her blankets were already on her bed. She hunched up under the covers, but she became more and more awake. At last she sat up. Mercy, it was *cold*. Was it morning yet? She turned on her bed lamp. No, her clock said it was only 4 A.M.

She heard rustlings in the hall and Dad saying "—see what's the matter with the furnace." His slippers flapped down the basement stairs. Katie snuggled back toward sleep. But the house didn't grow any warmer. There was more tramping on the basement stairs and Dad was growling to Mother that the furnace had broken down. Now doors were opening upstairs, more murmuring and questions and rustlings. The renters were awake. Katie heard Cousin Ben come trotting down the stairs, telling Dad he knew all about this blinkey old furnace, he'd helped Emily with it many a time.

He didn't seem able to fix it this time, though, for pretty soon Katie John heard Dad and Cousin Ben chopping wood in the basement. They must intend to build up fires in the fireplaces. Nearly every room in the house had a fireplace, and they would help keep the house warm until morning. However, Katie was too cold to wait. She trailed along the hall to her parents' bedroom across from the parlor and climbed in bed with Mother.

When she woke again she was alone in the big bed. The inside shutters were open, and cloudy daylight showed outside. A fire was leaping in the fireplace, but it barely took the chill off the air. Mother was phoning for a furnace man to come, and Dad was hurrying back and forth with more wood for the renters' fireplaces. In all the bustle the Tuckers didn't notice until Mother was clearing away the dishes that Cousin Ben hadn't come to the breakfast table.

"He's catching up on his sleep," Mother decided.

By mid-morning there was still no sign of life from Cousin Ben's room. Mother checked and found the old man still in bed, wheezing, with eyes fever bright.

"He's caught cold from all that running around in a chilly house last night," Mother reported. "I just hope it's nothing more than a cold."

She set Katie to fixing toast and juice on a tray and hurried to find the aspirin. At first Cousin Ben wouldn't let her take his temperature, but by late afternoon his wheezing was worse, the old man was weaker, and Mother insisted on putting the thermometer in his mouth. When she took it out, she went straight to the telephone and called the doctor.

Katie learned all this when she got home from school

as the doctor drove up. She waited in the second-floor hall with Dad while the doctor examined Cousin Ben. At last the doctor and Mother came out.

"It's pneumonia," the doctor said. "Not too bad yet, but with these old folks you never can tell. We'd better take him to the hospital."

The doctor phoned for an ambulance while Mother started bundling Cousin Ben up for his ride, over his weak protests that he wasn't going anywhere. Katie John tried to help and only managed to get in the way. The ambulance drove up with an important wail. It would all be exciting if it weren't that Cousin Ben looked so sick.

As the ambulance men took Cousin Ben out the front door, he wheezed to Mother, "Keep my room warm. I'll be back in a few days."

Mother twisted her hands with worry, but Dad tried to be hearty. "Don't worry, Abby. That old rooster is too tough to die."

Cousin Ben and Dad were right. In four days Cousin Ben was back home again. His eyes looked sunken, but the wheezing was gone, and he was just as talkative as ever. As Dad brought him in, Ben was telling all about the time his father had gotten pneumonia at the age of eighty-seven and lived to tell the tale.

Katie and Mother had been busy getting the Tuckers' downstairs bedroom ready for Cousin Ben. It would be a while before he was entirely well, and it would be easier for Mother to care for him down here than to run back and forth to the second floor with trays and medicine. The Tuckers would use the upstairs bedroom temporarily.

Cousin Ben sank into bed with a tired grunt. "Now then, Cousin Abigail, I'll write my sister Louisey to come up and take care of me. I won't have you frazzlin' yourself with a lot of nursing work."

Katie John stopped plumping pillows and looked to see what Mother thought of that idea. Mother looked horrified. Katie wondered why, and then realized that if sister Louisey came that meant one more room taken up that they couldn't rent and one more mouth to feed on the slender trickle of rent money they now had.

"No, no, Cousin Ben," Mother said hastily. "No need to bother your sister. Katie John and I will manage just fine."

Katie had started to think, "Poor Mother, with all this extra work of caring for an invalid." But at Mother's last words her thoughts changed abruptly: "Poor me."

Katie John glummed out of the room. She sat down on the bottom stair step and stuck her fingers up through her bangs. Work, work, and more work. At times like this she wished she had a sister to share in all the chores. What with helping with housework, keeping track of Buster, and taking care of Cousin Ben, she'd never have time for fun.

As Mother went back to the kitchen, Katie grumbled after her, "I might as well plan to be a housekeeper or a

nurse when I grow up. That's all I'm getting any practice at."

Mother replied gently, "Not all. You're getting practice at being a woman."

And for once Mother had the last word.

The Biggest Nobody
in Fifth Grade

Three things were wrong.

First, Cousin Ben kept opening his bedroom door. He was still in bed, recovering from pneumonia, but he was well enough to sit up and take notice of things. And every time Mother closed his door, Cousin Ben hopped out of bed and opened it again. He liked to sit propped up in bed and talk to everyone who passed in the hall. He had a fine view of all that went on because he still was occupying the Tuckers' downstairs bedroom, and his bed faced right toward the front hall.

It must look awful to everyone coming in the front door, Katie John thought. First thing they see when they come in the house is a talkety old man with a ragged beard sitting up in bed. No dignity to their house at all.

The second trouble was the two new renters, Gladys and Pearl. They were middle-aged women who worked at the egg factory. Actually it was an egg-packaging plant, but everyone called it the egg factory. Every evening, when the women came home, they turned on their radio full blast, and they listened to nothing but hillbilly music. The first night Katie John thought the music was gay, livened up the house. But now she was sick of the same old whang and whine of harmonicas and guitars and cowboy singers. Sometimes Gladys and Pearl forgot and left their radio on all day while they were at work, and it bothered Dad at his writing.

Dad finally had finished his novel about the newspaper business and mailed it off to a publisher. It was an exciting time now, waiting to see if the publisher would buy the book. Meantime Dad was trying to start a new book, but he was having a hard time of it, with that cowboy music blaring into his thoughts. He threatened to go in Gladys's and Pearl's room and turn the radio off when they forgot it, but so far he hadn't.

The worst thing, though, was what was happening at school. The kids were beginning to call Katie John "Teacher's Pet."

It was because Miss Howell lived at Katie's house, of course, and because sometimes they walked to school together. There wasn't a bit of truth to what the kids said. Miss Howell treated her just the same as she treated everyone else at school. In fact, it seemed as if Miss Howell gave her more extra work for whispering than she did anyone else. As to living in the same house with Miss Howell, well, it was true they had some good chats of an evening. But sometimes it was sort of uncomfortable, having your teacher right in the house with you. She knew whether you were getting your homework done or not.

Today Katie was walking to school alone. Miss Howell had to go early, and Sue was home with a runny nose. Katie John hurried along the frosty sidewalk, shivering at the cold. When she reached the school playground, however, she wondered why she'd hurried. With Sue absent, she had no one to stand around with before school. All the girls were paired off, best friends, or giggling in a bunch around Priscilla Simmons by the swings.

Katie leaned against the school wall. It was hard, getting to be one of a bunch when you're a newcomer in a small town. Besides, she'd been so busy helping at home she hadn't had much time to do things after school with girls, except Sue. Oh, the girls were all friendly enough, and she knew some of them at Campfire Girls, too. There had been a Campfire group in Barton's Bluff, after all. When she first came here she thought this poky little town wouldn't even have one. But all these girls had known each other since first grade. They had memories and jokes together from way back, and Katie John was still an outsider.

She could go and stand with Sally and Betsy Ann over there, but they were best friends. She'd just be an extra one. Thank the luck she had Sue for a best friend! Of course, everyone loved Sue, but until Katie had moved here, Sue had been the only girl in her neighborhood of old houses and old people, except for a few families with little children Buster's age, and Sue hadn't really paired off with anyone at school.

Katie John kicked her heel behind her on the wall she was leaning against and watched the girls swarming around Priscilla Simmons. Back home in California a lot of the girls used to stand around her that way. It felt strange to be just a nobody here.

"I'm the biggest nobody in the whole fifth grade," she muttered. She felt so cold and alone and sad that she could almost cry. Suddenly, thinking how things had been back in California, she remembered Juanita. Juanita was a Mexican girl who'd come to the fourth grade there in the middle of the year. She never had gotten to be good friends with anyone, and she always stood off by herself at recess. Now Katie knew how she must have felt. Nobody.

And it wasn't any better to be known as teacher's pet. You were still set off, apart. She ought to do something about that before everyone got it fixed in their minds. Maybe if she acted smart to Miss Howell, or didn't do her homework, or did something awful to Miss Howell. She could draw an ugly picture of the teacher on the blackboard. Or say! Put a mouse in Miss Howell's bed and tell about it at school. She could just imagine how Miss Howell would shriek, and . . .

Poor Miss Howell. Katie John was ashamed of herself. No, she wasn't going to do anything mean to her teacher just to get in good with the kids.

The bell rang then. Katie put off thinking about it until later and went in with the others.

The morning passed as usual until just before recess, when Miss Howell made an announcement. The Parent-Teacher Association in Barton's Bluff was sponsoring a concert Friday night to be given by a traveling ballet troupe. The troupe would dance the *Nutcracker Suite.* However, Miss Howell said, the ticket sale for the concert had not gone well so far, and the PTA was asking the school children to help sell tickets. As a reward, the class that sold the most tickets would receive a movie projector. Actually, the movie projector would belong to the whole school system, but it would stay with the winning class when not in use, and that class would see movies every Friday afternoon. After school Miss Howell would pass out tickets to those who wished to sell them.

At first Katie John didn't realize the full possibilities of the situation. She simply was entranced at the thought of seeing a ballet troupe dance that wonderful fairy tale about the nutcracker. She'd heard some of the music from the story, and especially loved "The Dance of the Sugar Plum Fairy." Oh, her folks just had to take her to the concert.

As the children marched out in line for recess, however, everyone was talking about the contest.

"What a chance to get out of work!" a big boy named Howard Bunch was saying. "Boy! Movies every Friday!"

"Probably the sixth grade will win. They think they're so big at everything."

"Or else some room at Jefferson School. Jefferson always wins stuff."

"My mother says if I bring home anything more to sell she'll brain me," one boy said. "I couldn't sell hardly any of those Christmas cards I ordered, and Mom had to pay for them."

Priscilla Simmons shrugged her shoulders delicately, saying, "I'd be afraid to go knocking on doors, asking strangers to buy tickets."

"Well, I wouldn't," Katie John spoke up. "I used to sell lots of tickets to school things back in California. All you have to do is believe people are going to want whatever you're selling."

"You mean just be brave?" someone asked.

"More than that," Katie explained. "When you go up to a door you think, 'This is Mrs. Jones' chance in a lifetime to see a ballet of the *Nutcracker Suite*.' And make her believe it, too."

Katie saw she had the attention of a number of her classmates. They'd paused around her before running out onto the playground. She felt a sudden glow at being the center of things.

"Yeah, but what if people say 'no,' anyway?"

"They never do," Katie bragged. "Not when I ask them. You kids just sell what you can, and don't worry,

I'll do the rest. I'll sell enough tickets so we'll win that movie projector. That's a promise."

Katie John had not told the exact truth. People had said "no" sometimes when she was selling tickets back home. Still, she had been unusually successful at selling tickets to school carnivals and church ham dinners. Certainly, here was her chance to be Somebody in the fifth grade. The boys and girls were looking at her with new respect and interest, and some of the girls walked out to the swings with her.

When Miss Howell handed out the tickets after school, Katie John insisted on taking a packet of fifty tickets. Then she raced home to tell Mother.

"Promise you'll buy three tickets for us to go?" she asked Mother breathlessly. "And tell all the renters when they get home from work not to buy tickets from any-one but me."

She was in a hurry to get out and start selling before any other school children began working her neighborhood. Buster was at loose ends, so she whirled him up with her—"Come on, Buster, you can help me sell tickets."

Cousin Ben was sitting up in bed, watching out his open bedroom door as usual, as they went by.

"What is it? What's going on?" he demanded.

But Katie called, "Can't stop. Tell you later," as she rushed Buster out the door.

Katie John rehearsed her sales approach. She would *not*

say, "You wouldn't want to buy a ticket, would you?" That was the way amateurs did it. No, she'd say, "How do you do? I'm Katie John Tucker. Have you ever gone to a ballet?" If the person said "No," she'd say, "Then now's your chance," and go on telling about it. If the person said "Yes," she'd say, "Then you know how much fun it is," and tell about the concert. Either way, she wouldn't mention a thing about tickets and their price until the very end, when she'd ask how many the person wanted.

There, that was the way to do it. She practiced her speeches on Buster, who wanted to know what the Nutcracker story was about, but she didn't have time to tell him now.

They started up a walk. Despite what Katie John had told her classmates about being confident, her hands were clammy. So much depended on her selling lots of tickets.

She rang the doorbell. A young woman came to the door, and Katie could hear a baby crying inside.

"How do you do? I'm Katie John Tucker. Have you ever been to a ballet?"

"Look, kid, are you selling something?" the woman said, looking over her shoulder as the baby wailed louder.

"Well—uh—"

"Because if you are, I don't want any. Oh, that baby— I've got to go." And the woman closed the door.

Katie went down the porch steps silently. Oh, well,

this was a freak case. Every house wouldn't have crying babies.

At the next house no one was home, or at least no one answered the door. On the corner was a large old home turned into apartments, like Katie's house. There'd be lots of buyers there. Unfortunately, the landlady wouldn't let Katie and Buster in, "to bother the renters," as the woman put it. And she had neither been to a ballet nor cared to go.

Up and down the street Katie John heard the same story: Either people didn't give two hoots about ballet dancers, or they kindly said they couldn't afford tickets. The rude ones didn't even hear her out. Times had been hard in Barton's Bluff, and no one had money to spare for "arty stuff," as one woman called it. "Now if it was a good minstrel show . . ." Katie gave her best sales talks, but it was hard to be bright and confident when she'd been told "no" seven, eight, nine times in a row. By dark she'd sold only three tickets, one to a sweet old lady and two to a young woman who said she and her husband had planned to go to the concert anyway.

Katie John dragged slowly through the dusk toward home. Buster said it was too cold to poke along, and ran home ahead of her. Katie was glad he was gone. She could feel the tears prickling close to falling. There was something awful about being rejected at door after door. She felt more Nobody than ever. And the kids at school were depending on her. She'd promised they'd win. What a fool she'd look, after her bragging.

A sob burped out of her throat. Stop it, she told herself fiercely.

At home, Mother and Dad bought three tickets and Mr. Peters very nicely took tickets for himself and Buster, even though he'd never heard of ballet dancers and seemed to have the idea he was going to see a school play. But that made only eight tickets she'd sold. None of the other renters would buy. Mr. Watkins reminded her that he had to work nights at the flour mill. A new man in the third floor, Mr. Peabody, just said "no," as did Gladys and Pearl.

"I bet they'd dig down in their purses fast enough if it was a hillbilly music show," Katie thought sourly.

The next day on the way to school Katie wondered how she could face the children when they asked how many tickets she'd sold. Sue was over her cold, and tried to console Katie that there was still one more day for ticket selling before the concert tomorrow night. Sue didn't have to worry, though. She had at least ten relatives who were sure to buy from her.

It was too drippy and cold to stand outside before school started. In the hall a fat girl named Rhoda Phillips came up to Katie.

"I tried your system and it worked," Rhoda said happily. "I believed in the ballet so hard I sold eleven tickets."

Katie forced a smile. "That's wonderful." She turned away before Rhoda could ask how many she'd sold. Then she stayed in the girls' rest room until the bell rang for classes to begin.

During school she kept her eyes on her books, and at recess she just nodded and tried to look gay and mysterious when people asked her how many tickets she'd sold so far.

Early in the afternoon the light rain turned to snow. It was the first snowfall of the year, but Katie John couldn't relish it as she watched the snowflakes drift against the windows. What if Mother wouldn't let her go out ticket selling in the snow? Oh, what a shame her first snow had to come at a time like this!

By the time school was out, however, the snow had stopped, leaving a light covering on the ground, and Mother said she could try to sell tickets if she'd be home before dark. Mother smiled at her brightly, as if she wanted to cheer Katie but secretly didn't think Katie would have much luck. Sue had to stay in her house because she was just over a cold, and Buster wanted to make a snowman, so this time Katie set out alone.

I've just got to sell tickets, Katie thought, even if I have to beg people, even if I have to give them . . . Oh, if only I could give them a bonus with each ticket. The way stores do at sales—something free with each purchase.

But she didn't have anything to give away. Katie scuffed through the soft snow. She wished she had time to play in it with Buster, but Dad said more snow was predicted tonight. Maybe it would still be on the ground Saturday. Maybe there'd be big drifts and Dad would let her shovel the walks, and . . .

Shovel the walks. Hmmm. Now there was an idea. Yes! She could offer to shovel walks free for every person who bought ballet tickets! Sure. People here were used to snow. They wouldn't think shoveling walks was fun, the way she did.

Katie's head came up and she gave a skip that kicked up the snow. Now she had a bonus offer. People would be sure to buy!

And Katie was right. By dark she'd sold twenty-seven tickets and promised to shovel the walks at nine houses, mostly homes of old people who found it hard to shovel snow. Many families had bought more than one ticket. Even old Miss Crackenberry had bought a ticket.

"How much are they?" she'd asked, when Katie made her offer. Upon learning that they were $1.50 apiece, Miss Crackenberry took one, saying that it would cost her that much to have a boy shovel the walk.

"But you come to my house first thing after school tomorrow," she'd told Katie John.

Katie had promised. Now she began to wonder how she'd get nine walks shoveled between after school and suppertime tomorrow. Oh, well, there wasn't much snow on the ground. And she'd get Buster to help her.

She ran home, jingling her pockets full of money. She banged the front door against the cold outside, and there

was Cousin Ben watching, like a spider waiting for a fly.

"Oh, Cousin Ben!" Katie cried. "I did it! I sold twenty-seven tickets today!" She poured the money out on his bed for him to see.

"Huh." He poked at the money. "How'd you do it? Thought nobody wanted to see bally dancers."

"I just offered to shovel snow for every family that bought tickets," Katie said, dancing around the bed. "Tomorrow after school I'm going to shovel walks at nine places."

Cousin Ben snorted. "No wonder. Cost 'em as much as a ticket to pay somebody to do it."

"That's what Miss Crackenberry said."

"Not surprised. Why, girl, you same as gave away

your tickets, when you figure you could have got paid for shoveling walks."

Trust Cousin Ben to pick out something wrong, trying to spoil things.

"That's the way I wanted to do it," she said stubbornly.

Now Cousin Ben added that he'd sold two tickets for her to the boy who delivered Miss Howell's groceries. So Katie couldn't really be mad at him. She smiled to herself as she imagined what had probably happened. The old man must have caught the boy as he went by the door and nearly talked him to death. The boy must have bought tickets just to get away.

Anyway, with Cousin Ben's two tickets and the eight she'd sold yesterday, that made thirty-seven tickets she'd sold altogether.

Next day at school Katie John had not one but two of those wonderful moments of triumph of the kind you remember forever.

On the playground before school a cluster of children were talking about how many tickets they'd sold—five, only three, seven. Katie and Sue joined the group. She'd already told Sue, but now she waited until someone asked, "How many did you sell, Katie John?"

Then, casually as a queen, she said, "Oh, thirty-seven."

"Thirty-seven! Wow!"

"Hey, I'll bet that does it for us!"

Some of the boys slapped her on the back and called her "good girl!" and even Priscilla Simmons sighed prettily that she just didn't see how Katie John could do it. Katie didn't tell her how, either.

The second and even better triumph came later in the morning when Miss Howell announced that the ticket sale count was in now from the schools, and her room had won the movie projector.

The girls shrieked and the boys yelled "Hurray!" pounding the floor with their feet. "Good old Katie!" someone yelled, and then it was "Hurray for Katie John!"

Katie John looked down, embarrassed and all a-prickle inside with delight. She knew she couldn't take all the credit, for the other children had done pretty well at selling tickets, too. Still, every time the movies were shown someone might remember that Katie John had helped win the projector.

Now she wasn't Teacher's Pet or Nobody. She was "Good Old Katie." Happily she stared out of the windows at the snowy playground.

Gradually, as the hubbub died down, she began to notice what she was looking at. Snow. Lots of snow. Great heaps of snow. Just as predicted, more snow had fallen during the night, and now it lay in heavy drifts on the ground. She'd been too excited about the tickets to pay much attention to it on her way to school.

Oh, great goodness. Those nine snowy walks weren't going to be easy to shovel this afternoon.

The Biggest Nobody
(Continued)

At recess Katie John confessed to Sue how she'd managed to sell so many tickets, and Sue promised to help her shovel snow. After school, however, Sue's mother said Sue could help only for a little while, because, after all, Sue was just getting over a cold.

The girls hurried to get shovels. Katie collected Buster and found a small gardening spade in the basement that was about his size.

"You want to help, don't you, Buster?" she asked on second thought.

"Sure," he agreed. If he couldn't play in water, messing with snow was the next best thing.

They all met on Miss Crackenberry's front walk. Her house sat close to the street, and the walk to her porch wasn't very long. They could clean it in no time, Katie and Sue told each other. The sun was shining, the air was crisp enough to break, like crackers, and the scrape of shovel on the cement walk made a bright ring. Soon the

children's cheeks were red and the snow was flying off the
walk to the sides.

Of course, Katie John had never shoveled snow before,
but by watching Sue for a few minutes she got the knack
of scoop and toss, without taking too heavy a load. At first
Buster wasn't much help. He said the snow was too heavy
for him to lift, and he kept throwing snowballs at the girls.
But Sue got a broom from her house and showed him
how to go along behind her and Katie, sweeping the
remains of the snow from the walk. Working together,
they reached the end of the walk in short order.

"There!" said Katie breathlessly. "Now for the next
place."

As they started to leave, Miss Crackenberry rapped on
a front window, then appeared at the door.

"Where are you going?" she called. "You haven't
done the sidewalk."

It seemed that she expected them to clean all of the
sidewalk that ran in front of her house along the street.
Katie John hadn't realized that property owners in snow
country are responsible for cleaning the public sidewalk
in front of their houses. When she'd promised to shovel
walks, she was thinking of the short front walks that ran
from the houses to the street.

"Oh, glory!" she groaned. "The sidewalks, too, in
front of eight more houses. Why, that'll take forever.
We'll never get done before dark."

Grimly Katie John set to work again. Scoop and toss,

scoop and toss. Her shoulders were beginning to ache, and she could feel a blister starting on her hand. It must be four o'clock now. The sun was low in the sky, and now it went under a cloud.

"I wish that sun would blaze out and melt this whole shebang!" Katie said. "Say, Sue, isn't there something that would melt this snow, something to do the job quicker than shoveling?"

Sue thought. "Well, there's rock salt, but I don't think it would work in snow this deep."

"What we need is a heat wave. Hey, I know. Why don't we pour hot water on the snow? That'd melt it fast enough."

Sue stared at Katie and giggled. "You get the craziest ideas. I don't know. I've never seen anybody clean his walk that way."

"We'll be pioneers then!" Katie laughed. "And I know just how to do it."

She ran home and got the coiled garden hose from its hook on the basement wall. In a few minutes she was back and hooking it up to the water faucet on the outside of Miss Crackenberry's house, down on the side foundation. Too bad it wasn't a hot-water faucet, but plain water ought to do it.

Katie turned on the water full force and aimed a strong spray from the hose at the snow. And it did work. Gradually the snow melted under the blast. Sue went along behind the spray, sweeping the melting snow off the walk.

Released of his duties, Buster followed Sue, happily stamping his snow boots in the water. In no time at all they had the walk clean.

"Katie, you're wonderful!" Sue exclaimed. "I think you've invented something."

Katie John grinned proudly. They could clean all the walks with the hose. Why, they'd be done in a whisk.

But just then Miss Crackenberry poked her head out of her door again. "Here, what's going on? Why is that water running? Oh, merciful heavens!"

She gave a little screech and ran out, pointing. "Look what you've done!"

The children looked back. The water was freezing into a thin sheet of ice on the sidewalk.

"Oh, no!" Katie wailed.

"Quick! Sprinkle rock salt on it," Miss Crackenberry cried.

She flew back to her house and brought out the salt. Then she stood over the girls as they sprinkled it on every bit of the ice.

When they'd fixed the sidewalk to her satisfaction, the old lady declared, "I should have known better than to have you do my walks, Katie John Tucker. I just hope that salt doesn't discolor the cement." She went back into her house. But the girls could see her still watching them from behind her front window curtains.

"Never even said 'thank you,'" Katie John said bitterly as she wound up the garden hose.

Sue looked at her watch. "It's almost four-thirty. In another hour or sooner it'll be dark. How are we going to get eight more walks done by then?"

"I don't know." Katie gave a weary sigh. "We'll just have to try."

The children put the hose back in Katie's basement. Then Buster deserted when he saw his warm apartment.

"I quit," he said flatly. "Dad'll be home pretty quick, and he's gonna make fried onions for supper."

Katie John pleaded with him and promised to make him an extra-wonderful treasure hunt tomorrow. Buster just went into his apartment and banged the door after him. To make matters worse, when the girls went past Sue's house, Mrs. Halsey called out that Sue must come in after she helped with one more sidewalk.

The other shoveling jobs were in a neighborhood a few blocks away. The girls hurried as fast as they could, dragging their shovels in the snow. At the first house they had a pleasant surprise. The man of the house hadn't wanted to wait until afternoon to have his walks cleaned and had already done them himself. The next place was a fairly easy one, too, for the house sat close to the street on a narrow lot, so that neither the walk to the door nor the public sidewalk was very long. Katie and Sue plunged at shoveling. All the fun had gone out of the work, but they soon had the walk cleared.

Six more to go. And the next place would take forever. Katie straightened her aching back and groaned as she looked at the long sidewalks of the big house on its wide, gracious lot.

Just then Buster came running. "Been looking for you," he puffed. "Your ma says tell you people been calling at your house, wanta know why you don't come shovel their snow. But she says for you to come home when it gets dark. You gotta eat and get ready to go to the bally show. Me, too." This being the longest speech Buster had made yet to Katie, he puffed some more, then started to trot off. He turned to yell over his shoulder, "Your ma says you can finish tomorrow."

Katie almost sobbed. "But I promised people I'd do the walks today. Besides, it might snow more tonight. I'd have mountains of snow to shovel tomorrow."

Sue looked sadly at her friend. "Poor Katie."

She stayed to help Katie, even though it went against her grain to disobey her mother.

"Hey, you girls. Getting paid for that?"

Katie and Sue lifted sore necks and saw three boys from their room at school walking down the middle of the snowy street. They were Howard Bunch, the biggest boy in the class, a little one named Sammy, and Pete Hall-strom. Howard was a bulky boy with red cheeks and straight black hair. Peter was almost as tall as Howard and looked taller because he was skinny. Sammy ran between them like a frisky little terrier.

Katie shook her head in answer and wished they'd go on. But the boys lingered to watch the girls' shovels work.

"Look at that," Howard said. "They handle their shovels like croquet mallets."

"Hey, Katie," Sammy yelled. "You threw that shovelful back on the sidewalk."

"They're digging for gold. Come on, Sue, gimme a piece of gold." That was Pete.

"Why don't you go on, if you can't think of anything funny to say?" Katie snapped. She shoveled harder.

"Didja ever see anybody work so slow?" Pete jeered. "Why, I could shovel faster than that and eat an apple at the same time."

Howard said, "I could shovel faster than that and read a comic book."

Sammy said, "I could shovel faster than that and—and—"

Katie John stopped and stared down at her shovel, trying to keep from throwing it at those dumbbells. Suddenly she looked up with a glint in her eye.

"Maybe Sammy could do it faster, but Howard and Pete couldn't," she declared.

"Whaddya mean?" Howard said, stung. "I'm bigger than them."

"But Sammy looks stronger," Katie said. "I bet he could do this whole big piece of sidewalk before you could do that little part over there."

"Yeah!" Sammy said rashly.

"You're crazy," Howard told him.

"You say!" Sammy grinned.

"Gimme that shovel." Howard grabbed it out of Katie's hands. "All right, big mouth, we'll just see!"

"Right!"

Sammy seized Sue's shovel and tore away at the long stretch of snow, while Howard made the snow fly from the short patch. Katie looked at Sue, trying to keep her face straight. She was afraid that if she laughed Pete would see and catch on. In a few minutes Howard had finished his piece. Sammy hadn't cleared all of his part, but he'd done so much that it looked as though he'd actually done more than Howard.

"Maybe Sammy couldn't do it all," Katie said, to keep things going, "but he still worked faster than you did, Howard."

"He did not!" Howard said angrily, while Sammy finished off his section in a spray of snow.

"The only way you can really prove it is to time your work," said Sue, doing her part. "I've got a watch."

"Oh, they're all tired out now." Katie John smiled in a particularly maddening way.

"Who's tired?" Howard yelled. "Maybe Sammy. Not me."

"All right then," said Katie, "each of you do part of the sidewalk down at this house and we'll time you." It was her next shoveling job.

"Me, too," Pete said eagerly. "I can do better than either of them."

Shovels scraped, boys grunted, and the snow flew. Sue

held her watch and timed five-minute contests, Howard against Sammy, Sammy against Pete, Pete against Howard. By the time they'd cleared the walks at that place and the one next door Sue declared Howard the winner. But little Sammy had done better than Pete, so that made Sammy happy, too. Pete started to grouch, but Sue whispered something in his ear that spread a silly grin over his face.

"Okay, you were right," Katie John told the boys generously. "You all can shovel faster than we can. Anyway, thanks a lot for the help." To Sue she added, "You'd better go on home now, or your mother will be mad. I'm rested, and I've only got three more places to do."

"What help?"

"Three more places? You getting paid for cleaning these walks?" Pete asked.

"If you are, we ought to get a cut for helping," Howard added.

"Yeah!"

"Why, you ungrateful things!" Sue exclaimed. "She's not getting paid a cent. She's doing it for you, actually."

Katie tried to shush Sue. She didn't want the story going around school about how she'd sold all those tickets, after her big talk about her sales system. But Sue went right on telling how Katie John had brought all this work on herself just to help their room win glory and the movie projector.

"Well." "Huh." The boys had their heads down, finding something very interesting in the snow to poke at with their boot toes.

Finally Pete looked straight at Katie. "You're a good sport, Katie John Tucker."

"You're all right," Sammy said.

"Hey, look, it's almost dark." Howard talked fast. "If you've got three more places to do, you won't get done in time for the concert. We'll help you, huh, you guys?"

The boys ran home to get shovels, promising to come right back. Sue had to leave, but she said she'd stop at Katie's house and tell her mother that Katie would be along pretty soon.

Katie John waited alone in the chill dusk. Her back ached, her neck ached, her shoulders ached, the backs of her legs were stripes of pain, she had three broken blisters on her hands. And she felt wonderful. Today she'd been called "good old Katie," "hurray for Katie," and now "good sport." What more could a nobody ask?

The sky was completely black and the street lights were on before Katie and the boys finished the sidewalks. Still, she was able to eat supper and get to the high-school auditorium with her parents in time for the opening curtain.

When the house lights dimmed, Katie John leaned back in the dark and breathed deep and slow as she watched the colorful dancers through a happy haze. She was so tired it was like watching a ballet in a dream. Possibly the nicest way of all to watch a ballet troupe dance a fairy tale, she thought contentedly.

Cousin Ben's Door

"Talk about big winds, say!" Cousin Ben's chin whiskers were waggling away. "One time down home they came up the Big Wind of '16 that blew everything cat-west. Pigs, cats, rain barrels, everything that wasn't tied down went sailing. That wind played whaley with old Joe Tasket's bees, too."

"Your move, Cousin Ben," Katie John said.

They were playing checkers on Cousin Ben's bed, or at least they were supposed to be playing checkers, but mostly Cousin Ben was talking. He went right on.

"Them bees was just a-fixing to swarm, when this wind came whooshing up, scattered them and their queen all over Cooper County. They say down there they's still mixed-up, lonesome bees trying to find their way back home to Joe Tasket's hives."

Katie John laughed in spite of herself. Cousin Ben did tell good stories.

"Your move," she repeated.

After all his talking, maybe he'd make a mistake on the checkerboard. But Cousin Ben was a sly one. Somehow during his story he'd noticed the threatening move she'd made.

"We-l-l, I'll just go this way," Cousin Ben said. "Hop, hop, *and* hop."

Katie John looked at the board in dismay as he took her last three checkers.

"I win," he chuckled. "Play again?"

"Oh, all right."

She was supposed to be entertaining Cousin Ben so he wouldn't bother people. He still kept his door open and talked to everyone who came in the front door. Poor Miss Julia had to listen to him quite a bit. Every time she crept past his door, he started talking to her, and the little woman was so shy, Katie thought, that she never had the nerve to put a word in edgewise and get away. Usually someone had to rescue her.

Last night something had happened that made Dad angry with Cousin Ben. Two of the third-floor rooms were still unrented, so Dad had put a sign down by the bridge, advertising rooms for tourists. Last night, for the first time, a family of tourists had come to the house. But Cousin Ben had talked to them so much when they came into the hall that the woman in the family had said she was too tired to stand talking to "a garrulous old man" all night, and she'd marched the whole family back to their car and left. Dad had spoken sharply to Cousin Ben then, but the old man insisted, as he always did, that someone else had left his door open.

The Tuckers were beginning to wonder whether Cousin Ben would ever get out of bed. He'd been home from the hospital for two weeks now, but every time Mother tried to persuade him to sit up in a chair for a while, Cousin Ben said he felt a chill coming on again. He was taking awfully good care of himself, because he said he still wasn't "over the hump." He often pointed out that there'd been no snow here at Christmastime, and "a green Christmas means a white graveyard," meaning, Katie supposed, that a lot of people would die this winter. She didn't think he had to worry; he looked even more chipper now than the day he'd arrived.

Almost every day, however, Cousin Ben put on a pitiful voice, saying, "If I can just get past February, maybe I'll be good for another year."

And the Tuckers worried, "Heavens, does he mean to stay in bed all through February, too?"

Privately, Katie John thought Cousin Ben was having the time of his life, lying there in bed being waited on. If she had her way, they'd simply tell Cousin Ben they had to rent this room now. But Mother wouldn't do it. She said that, after all, it was their fault, or, rather, their furnace's fault, that he'd gotten pneumonia, and they couldn't put him out until he was all well.

Which he never will be at this rate, Katie thought, banging a checker over Cousin Ben's king.

There was a rustle and a whispering in the hall. Buster peered around the corner of the open door. He motioned, and a boy and a girl smaller than he appeared and stared into the room at Cousin Ben. They didn't speak, just looked and looked at Cousin Ben. The little girl put her finger in her mouth and her face puckered.

"What do you want?" Cousin Ben asked sharply. "Speak up."

The little girl shook her head, looking as if she were about to cry. Finally the boy said, "Are you ever going to get well?"

Ha, thought Katie. That's what we'd like to know.

"I don't know," the old man snapped. "Haven't got past February yet. Now scat."

"What's the matter with the young'uns around here?" Cousin Ben complained to Katie John. "Almost every day Buster drags in different neighbor children, and all they do is stand and stare at me and worry about my health."

At first, he said, he thought it was nice of them to ask how he was, but now they gave him "the willies."

"Way they stand around with their long faces makes me think maybe I *will* die."

He kicked fretfully under his covers, and the checkers slid off the board. Katie decided it was a good time to end the game.

"I'm sorry," she told him. "I'll ask Buster what it's all about."

She pulled the door shut after her as she went out of the room. A demon came into her, and she waited silently outside the door, with her hand on the doorknob. Sure enough, there was a creak of Cousin Ben's bed, and then the knob turned under her hand as Cousin Ben pulled the door open a crack. Katie John yanked it shut again. The knob rattled, but she held tight. A snort sounded on the other side of the door, and then the bed creaked again.

Katie snickered. Cousin Ben couldn't say someone had left his door open this time.

Mother came along just then, but fortunately didn't notice what Katie had been doing. She looked too weary to notice anything.

"Honey, I'm going to bed," she said. "I feel miserable, and I think I'm coming down with the flu. Will you help Dad fix supper?"

Goodness, Mother *must* be sick. Katie couldn't remember that her mother had ever gone to bed before ten o'clock at night. She wanted to bustle around Mother with a hot-water bottle and a thermometer, but Mother said she only wanted to crawl into bed and be left alone. So Katie went off to find Dad and help cook something for supper.

Later Dad took Mother's temperature, and found it was running high. She had the flu, all right. He called the doctor for some medicine, and then he and Katie got some food onto the table. They managed pretty well with wieners and canned vegetables. When Cousin Ben heard that Mother was sick, he made the supreme sacrifice and said maybe he could make it to the table, to save extra work of carrying a tray to him.

The three of them sat down to their wieners, Cousin Ben in his bathrobe, snorting a little when he looked at Katie, but not saying anything about their door-tugging episode. The doctor had said Mother probably would be all right if she spent the next few days in bed, but it was a glum meal table without her to hear all their news. Katie John felt even more gloomy when she began to wonder how they'd get the work done without Mother.

It was amazing how much work there was to running an apartment house. It took all three of the Tuckers to keep it going. Mother did the cleaning and laundry for the men's rooms—the lady renters took care of their own rooms—besides her own housework in the Tuckers' part of the house, and Katie John helped her three afternoons after school and on Saturday mornings. Dad wrote in his room until the middle of the afternoon, and then he did the heavy work of caring for the old house—shoveling walks, making repairs, stoking the furnace, chopping kindling for the renters' fireplaces, emptying the renters' wastebaskets.

And then there were all the interruptions from the renters. Seemed as if every time the Tuckers sat down for supper, Pearl or Gladys needed change for a quarter for the gas meter on their cookstove. Or the light bulb in Mr. Peabody's room was burned out. Or Mr. Watkins wanted to pay his rent. (The Tuckers would have welcomed that kind of interruption from Mr. Peabody, for he was two weeks behind on his rent.)

"How are we going to get all the work done?" Katie said to Dad finally. "Day after tomorrow is Saturday, the day Mother and I clean the rooms and change the beds."

"Oh, don't worry, Katykins," Dad said. "I'll quit writing for a while and do it."

"Work's what makes the world go around," Cousin Ben observed.

"I thought it was love that made the world go around," Dad said.

"Wouldn't know about that. Been a bachelor all my life."

Katie sighed. It was a shame that Dad would have to stop writing right now. His new book—he wouldn't tell them what it was about—was going so well. By the time she left for school each morning, his typewriter was rattling away like a hailstorm.

Besides, Dad had never done housework. She couldn't imagine him vacuuming rugs, tidying up, or running the washing machine and the ironer in the basement. Katie realized, to her pleased surprise, that she knew more about cleaning and washing and ironing than Dad did. She did not, however, relish the idea of doing mountains of housework all weekend long. Even with Dad trying to help, it would be a miracle if they got everything done. Well, the important thing was for Mother to get well without worrying about things. Katie John washed the supper dishes so Dad could take care of Mother.

Next day, Friday, on the way to school, Katie told Sue about the current Tucker crisis.

"I wish we could afford to hire a cleaning woman," she said, "so Dad wouldn't have to quit writing."

Anyway, she added, she was going to do as much as she could. She'd have to skip the Campfire Girls' meeting after school to hurry right home.

Then it was that Sue the follower, Sue the quiet one, Sue, the one who always said, "You're wonderful, Katie," Sue had the brilliant idea.

"Why don't you get the Campfire Girls to help you?" she asked.

Katie stared at her friend bundled round as a bear in her snow suit.

"But—why would they want to help?"

"For their honor points," Sue explained. "We all have to help somebody to get those points, so why not get them for helping you?"

"Why—yes! With all those girls, we could swarm all over the house, get the work done in no time. We could make a regular party of it." Katie hugged Sue. "Sue, that's a wonderful idea!"

Sue turned red with the delight of being the idea-person. But she said, practically, that they'd better wait to see whether the girls would do it, and whether Mrs. Wowski, their Campfire leader, would approve of the plan.

Before school Katie and Sue talked to some of the girls about the idea, and the girls were quite agreeable to it.

Betsy Ann and Sally said they'd been wanting to see Katie John's old house, anyway. Katie hesitated to mention the plan to Priscilla Simmons, though. Priscilla's folks were rich, and Priscilla might turn up her pretty nose at the thought of cleaning an apartment house.

After school at the Campfire meeting, Mrs. Wowski said Sue's idea was "just grand."

"I've been trying to think of a good work project for you girls," she said, "and the need at Katie's house certainly fits the bill."

Even Katie could win her honor point if she worked extra hard, Mrs. Wowski added.

Katie John promised, and looked across the room to see what Priscilla Simmons thought of it all.

Priscilla was tossing back her curls and saying to the girl next to her, "Isn't it nice that we can help people who are really in need?"

Katie John chewed her lower lip. When Mrs. Wowski had spoken of the need at Katie's house, it had sounded all right. But Priscilla made it sound as if she were going out with a Christmas basket for the poor folks. Well, wait till Priscilla Simmons saw her house. The old Clark place might not be as grand as Priscilla's house on Partridge Avenue, but still it was beautiful inside, Katie thought, with its gleaming banisters and antique furniture and fireplaces in every room.

And a wispy-bearded old man propped up in a rumpled bed right by the front door. Oh, dear! She'd forgotten about Cousin Ben. And he'd talk and talk. What would Priscilla think? And the other girls, for that matter. None of them had ever been to Katie's house before. Cousin Ben would give the impression that the Tuckers' house was a sloppy rooming house.

"Is that all right, Katie?" Mrs. Wowski was asking.

"What?"

"I said," the leader repeated, "that the girls would meet at your house at nine o'clock tomorrow morning with their dust rags. You show them what to do, and they'll help you all day until the work is done."

"Well—yes," Katie said, then, realizing she sounded reluctant, tried to put more enthusiasm into her "Thank you, Mrs. Wowski."

After the meeting the eight girls crowded around her, chattering about how fast they could work, and could they see the dumb waiter that Katie John once got stuck in, and wouldn't it be fun, working all together? Katie John put on a cheerful face and said, "Oh, yes" and "Good," but all the time she was thinking, "Oh, dear. What to do about Cousin Ben?"

Later, as Katie and Sue walked home, Sue asked, "What's the matter, Katie?" She could tell something was wrong.

Katie started to tell her, then closed her mouth. No use worrying Sue about it. There was nothing she could do. Besides, she didn't like to talk about being ashamed of Cousin Ben, even to Sue. Actually, she wasn't ashamed of him, she told herself. It was just how he looked there with his bedroom door open, the first thing the girls would see when they came into the house. If only he'd keep his door shut. But he wouldn't. As soon as he heard the girls coming, he'd be sure to want to see what all the commotion was about.

Maybe I could lock him in, Katie thought desperately. Or beg him not to open his door. But no, that would hurt his feelings if he thought I was ashamed of him.

Oh, goodness, she wished Mother had never gotten sick.

Katie John told Sue good-by at Sue's house and walked on through the early dusk toward her house. Yellow light shone out from nearly every window of the square brick house. Usually it cheered her to see the house all lit up when she came home, and to think that each light meant a renter home for the night and sheltered under the flat roof. Tonight the lights didn't mean a thing. There was only one hope. Maybe Mother would be well suddenly, and the girls wouldn't have to come, after all.

Katie John went straight to her mother's room, but of course Mother wasn't well yet. Her face looked gray, and she said her head hurt so. Katie brought her some water and an aspirin. Then she got the vacuum cleaner and took it to Cousin Ben's room. There was still half an hour before she and Dad needed to start supper; she could clean Cousin Ben's room now, so that at least the girls wouldn't have to do that tomorrow.

Cousin Ben's door was open, as usual, for all the world to see, and his room looked just awful—dirty socks on the floor, sticky medicine bottles all over his bedstand, his worn blue bathrobe falling off a chair, the evening paper scattered over his bed. Ben Orlick was leaning against his pillows, working the crossword puzzle. *Before Dad can ever get to it,* Katie thought. Dad liked to relax with the crossword puzzle every evening.

When Katie John dragged the vacuum cleaner through the doorway, Cousin Ben looked up. "What are you bringing that thing in here for?" he complained. "Man can't think."

Katie John shoved up her bangs. All right. The way he acted, and the way his room looked, she'd just say it. Come right out and tell him to keep his door shut tomorrow.

"Cousin Ben," she began.

Children's voices sounded on the porch. That was Buster, saying, "Come on. He's in here." Feet rattled on the porch steps, the front door opened, and Buster tiptoed in, followed by three small boys and a tiny girl. All five children crowded into the open doorway of Cousin Ben's room. "Ssh!" Buster was whispering. The children stopped scuffling and stood motionless, wide eyes on the old man in the bed.

The girl took a quick little breath. "I see his beard," she whispered.

"Where's his sack?" a boy asked Buster.

Suddenly the little girl ran to the bed and threw her arms around Cousin Ben's neck.

"Oh, poor Santy Claws," she wailed, "are you going to die?"

Katie's hand flew to her mouth, and then she burst into laughter. She couldn't help it. "Haw, haw, haw!" Great belly laughs rolled out. So that was it! That crazy Buster still thought Cousin Ben was Santa Claus, and he'd been going around telling all the little kids that Santa Claus was sick at his house.

The children stared at her, shocked. One little boy ran over and kicked her on the ankle.

"What's the matter, you want Santy to die?" he growled.

"Oh! Oh, I'm sorry!" Katie gasped, wiping tears of laughter from her eyes. "I'm sorry, but—"

Cousin Ben was trying to pry the little girl loose from his neck. His face was red, either from anger or embarrassment or because the child was choking him.

"I'm not Santa Claus!"

"He just says that because it's a secret," Buster explained to his friends.

Cousin Ben pushed the girl away. "I tell you I'm not— All of you—clear out of here—"

"I never knew Santa Claus was such a mean old man," one boy muttered, while the little girl began to sob, "Santy Claws mean."

Cousin Ben stopped yelling. He looked at the chil-

dren's unhappy faces. And he knew he was licked. He was giving Santa Claus a bad name.

"All right. All right now," he said in a sudden sweet voice that started up the giggles in Katie again. He glared at her and continued, "Now, then, children, you just go along and don't worry about good old Santa Claus. He'll be around next Christmas with his bag full of toys, ho, ho."

The little girl began to smile through her tears, and the boys' faces cleared up. Cousin Ben climbed out of bed and herded them through the doorway, giving jolly "ho-ho's" that made Katie snort with suppressed laughter.

"Just leave me alone," he told Buster, "so I can get well, ho, ho."

He closed the door smartly after the children.

"Pesky young'uns," he muttered, not meeting Katie John's eyes as he got back in bed. "Next thing they'll be wanting presents."

Katie gulped down her giggles. Poor old Cousin Ben. He was so embarrassed. She began to wind up the vacuum cord. She wouldn't bother him now. Ben called after her, "Close the door. Everybody leaves my door open—pack of young'uns stare at me like I'm something in a zoo. Keep my door shut now, you hear!"

Katie closed the door and tore down the hall for the kitchen. She could feel another big belly laugh coming on, and she wanted to enjoy it.

So the Problem of the Open Door was solved. Next day, when the Campfire Girls came, Cousin Ben's door stayed shut tight as a safe.

As for the cleaning work, the old house had never held such a whoop and chatter and skirmish as the girls chased every bit of dirt in their paths. And with all their work, the girls still found time for fun. When sheet-washing time came, Katie John discovered that the old washing machine in the basement swished with a fine rhythm. All the girls danced to the washing machine as it cheerfully pounded away—tump-tump ti-*ump*-tump, tump-tump ti-*ump*-tump!

Hot-Potato Katie

The only bare spot on Katie John was her eyes, and they smarted and watered with the cold. It was a bitter February morning, with the sun only a faint spot in the dull sky. Banks of snow edged the sidewalks as Katie and Sue hurried to school bundled in their snow suits and mittens. Katie had pulled her hood low over her forehead and tied a muffler across her face. Already the muffler was wet and nasty from breathing through the wool, but it was better than leaving her nose and mouth exposed to the freezing air.

Inside her wrappings, however, she was toasty warm, for Katie John had figured out a way to beat the cold. She was loaded with hot potatoes.

Mother had given her the idea. Last night, when California-born Katie was complaining of the cold, Mother had told how she'd kept warm on the way to school when she was a little girl. She'd carried a hot baked potato in each mitten. So Katie had decided if potatoes would keep her hands warm, why not potatoes for the rest of her? Early this morning she'd put ten little potatoes in the oven.

And now the potatoes were warming her, like so many little heating pads. She had potatoes in her pockets, potatoes at the ankles of her snow suit, potatoes inside her jacket, potatoes in her mittens, and even a hot potato at the back of her neck, held in place by her muffler.

"You ought to try it," she told Sue. "I'm as warm as a—as a potato in an oven."

Sue was all hunched together against the cold with her hands inside her sleeves, but she said doubtfully, "What are you going to do with all those potatoes when you get to school?"

"Maybe I'll eat 'em for lunch." Katie laughed.

Good ideas—when they worked—always made her feel perky. And this idea certainly was working. She swung along, free and easy, not bothered by the freezing air, while Sue trotted beside her, huddled in her snow suit. Why, as long as the potatoes in the cellar held out, she'd stay warm all winter!

Katie and her hot potatoes created quite a sensation at school. When she and Sue arrived, the little hall next to the fifth-grade classroom was full of boys and girls hanging up their wraps or sitting on the floor tugging at stubborn snow boots. Chatter filled the air: "Wow, it's cold today," and "I think my nose is frozen stiff," and "I'm *all* frozen."

"Not me," Katie John declared. "See?"

She flung open her jacket, and the potatoes fell out on the floor.

"Potatoes!"

The boys snatched them up. "Hey, they're hot! Catch!" The potatoes flew from boy to boy.

"I wasn't a bit cold," Katie boasted to the children crowding around her. She pulled off her snow pants, more potatoes rolled out, and the girls squealed with laughter.

"Depend on Katie John!"

"Say, that's an idea!"

But, "My father brought me to school in the car with the heater on," Priscilla Simmons said softly. Her skirt was fresh and unrumpled by confining snow pants. "I still think that's the best way."

And now Katie was discovering to her dismay that some of the potatoes had broken open in her snow suit. She had mealy flecks of potato all over her skirt and blouse and even in her hair where the potato had been at the back of her neck.

"Hey, potato for breakfast!" Howard Bunch yelled. "Get the butter."

The boys jostled Katie, pretending they were salting her, picking pieces of potato off of her and eating them.

"Boy, does she taste good!"

"Good old Hot-Potato Katie!"

"Don't." Katie pushed at the boys. She saw Priscilla standing there looking so—so ladylike. Suddenly things had become a bit too hearty to suit Katie John.

"Oh, go on," she told the boys, twitching away from them. "Stop it."

She ran to the girls' rest room to finish picking the potato from her clothes. The fat girl named Rhoda Phillips followed her.

"My, Katie John, you sure are popular with the boys," she said. "I bet you get lots of valentines this Friday."

"Oh, boys!" Katie scowled. "Who cares about valentines from boys!"

"I know, boys are awful," Rhoda agreed. "But you care on Valentine's Day. Usually Priscilla Simmons gets the most valentines. All the boys think she's so sweet."

Rhoda explained the custom at this school. Everyone's valentines were placed in a basket on the teacher's desk. Then after lunch Miss Howell would call out the names on the cards and the children would go up and get them.

"Priscilla always goes up for valentines the most," Rhoda sighed.

"Well, I don't want any valentines from any dumb old boys," Katie John said, brushing off her skirt and heading for the classroom.

But deep down she knew she did. All morning during reading and penmanship and the test on state capitals she kept thinking about this valentine business. Why, if everybody saw you going up for valentines, it would be a disgrace if you didn't get any from boys at all. At recess she asked Sue about it.

"Yes, it's the valentines from boys that count," Sue said. "I heard Miss Howell tell my mother she thought it was cruel to hand out valentines in front of the whole class, but that's the way it's always been done at this school. And that's the way kids want it, really."

Sue didn't have to worry, anyway, Katie thought. She was sure to get a valentine from her friend, Bob. Probably from other boys, too, because Sue was sweet, the same way Priscilla Simmons was sweet. Per-Simmons, Katie thought. Silly Simmons. But the names didn't fit, much as she wished they did. Priscilla was little and pretty, with fair silky curls and brown eyes. And she wasn't smarty, either. That wasn't why she made Katie John uncomfortable. It was just that Priscilla was so— right. Never flustered, or red-sweaty-faced, always sure that people liked her. She came from an old Barton's Bluff family, she was pretty, and you just knew she'd sail through life like a beautiful white swan.

I bet every boy in the room gives her a valentine, Katie gloomed.

Just then the boys came galumphing up to Katie John.

"Here's the potato girl!" they yelled. "Hot-Potato Katie!"

"Hey, we're hungry!"

"Yum-yum!"

They pretended to pick pieces of potato off of her and made loud smacking sounds of eating.

Katie John flailed at the air, trying to brush the boys away.

"Cut it out!" she yelled. But the boys laughed and

scuffled around her the more. Then the bell rang and she escaped.

Katie's lips were set in a straight line as she got in line to march into class. One thing she knew for sure: boys didn't give valentines to girls they scuffled with. Oh, sure, they liked Katie. Katie was a good old pal. But when it came time for lace valentines, it was the sweet girls that boys thought of.

It's my own fault, Katie thought bitterly. I act like a tomboy, so boys treat me like a tomboy. Wearing potatoes to school! Potato meal all over me, for goodness' sakes! Why did I have to do such a dumb thing?

After school, when she told Mother about it, she repeated, "Why do I do things like that? Other girls don't do crazy things." She sighed. "Only, my ideas don't seem crazy at first. They just seem like good ideas."

"Did the potatoes keep you warm?" Mother asked.

"Yes, but—"

"Well, then, it *was* a good idea, wasn't it?"

"At first," Katie John admitted. "But the potatoes broke, and the boys laughed and—well, all I know is, Priscilla Simmons would never get into a mess like that. Why do I?"

"Because you've got a wonderful imagination, Katie," Mother said, smoothing down Katie's bangs. "And your imagination is going to take you into far places all your life. It may get you into some messes, but it will bring you greater joys, too. Priscilla's life may be smoother than yours, but don't you suppose it's a little dull?"

"No," Katie said, and she went away because she didn't want to talk about it any more.

She was tired of leading a rumpled life. Katie John studied herself in the mirror in her room: hair flying out like sticks, freckles, messy-looking old jumper with a piece of potato skin still clinging, blouse tail hanging out.

"Rumpled-stiltskin," she said in disgust.

It was time for a change. After all, she'd be eleven next month. From now on she was going to be a lady. She'd tie her hair back with a ribbon, and she'd wear her prettiest dresses. Katie went to the closet to pick out a school dress for tomorrow. She shoved the hangers about.

"I haven't even *got* a pretty dress."

Of course, that was her fault, too. She'd never bothered about clothes. At Christmastime she'd scorned the girls who were asking for dresses and finery. She had wanted interesting presents, such as books and an army cot for camping out in the orchard next summer. Why ask for clothes when you knew your folks would provide something to cover you, anyway? So now that's all she had: neat skirts and blouses to cover her, nothing exciting.

Well, she'd ask Mother to make her something pretty. Meantime, she'd wear her best dress tomorrow. And a ribbon to match—if she could find one. Katie John rummaged through her drawer and came upon a slender gold bracelet that had been Great-Aunt Emily's. She'd wear that, too.

And she'd speak softly and smile sweetly and walk with the girls like a lady.

And I'll change my name, Katie thought suddenly. Katie John was a tomboy name. It fairly sounded brisk and freckle-faced. "Katherine," she tried the sound of it, "Cathy." Yes, that was it, "Cathy." It had a smooth, soft sound.

The next day on the way to school she instructed Sue, "From now on, call me Cathy."

Sue giggled. "It doesn't sound like you at all. I'll forget."

"Well, it's going to sound like the new me. Now you do it."

At school she asked Miss Howell to call her Cathy, but Miss Howell said she was already down on the school rolls as Katie John. Why not wait until next fall and register as Cathy if she still wanted to then, her teacher suggested, smiling, so Katie had to be satisfied with that. Anyway, people would get in the habit of calling her Cathy if Sue did it all the time.

The only trouble was, Sue kept forgetting. At recess she said, "Come on, Katie—I mean Cathy," and the other girls stared at Katie John.

The boys and some of the girls were building a snow fort on the playground.

"Look at those tomgirls," Katie John said in her new soft voice.

She stayed on the sidewalk, standing with Sue and Priscilla and a few other girls. It was cold standing still, especially as she hadn't worn her snow pants today because she didn't want to rumple her best dress. She slid the gold bracelet down to her wrist.

"Did you ever see my bracelet?" she said politely to Priscilla, holding out her arm.

"Oh, it's pretty." Priscilla admired it. "I just love antiques."

Katie didn't know whether that was a compliment or an insult. It was hard to talk in this sweet, polite way to Priscilla and her friends. Whoops of excitement rang from the snow fort as a snowball battle began. It looked like fun—no, it wasn't. It wasn't ladylike.

"Come on, Katie John," Howard Bunch was yelling.

Katie smiled her new smile and shook her head. She turned to listen to the girls' chatter.

All through the day she was Cathy, sitting down carefully at her desk so as not to wrinkle the back of her dress, smoothing her hair back under the green ribbon. But the boys didn't even seem to notice. At the lunch hour when Howard and Pete asked if she was coming to the fort, Cathy said "no" and started to say something gentle, but the boys ran on before she could say it.

Well, then, she'd just make them notice Cathy. The

children had to stay in their classroom at afternoon recess because it was sleeting. Cathy went up to Howard.

She slid the bracelet on her wrist and asked nicely, "What do you want to be when you grow up?"

"A jet pilot. Eeerrrrr." He veered away, swooping with his arms a-tilt.

How could boys notice her if they wouldn't even stand still? Cathy swished her skirts over to Pete Hallstrom.

"Pete, what do you want to be when you grow up?"

Pete was glueing a part to a model car. "Can't talk," he muttered, not looking up from his delicate work.

Sammy and Bob were chasing Sue with a blackboard eraser.

"Sammy," Cathy said in her dear little lady voice, "what do you want to be when you grow up?"

Sammy stopped. "Gonna run my dad's shoe store, what else?" He looked at Cathy smoothing down her skirts. "Whatcha all dressed up for? Going somewhere after school?"

But before she could answer he tore away after Sue again. Well, at least he'd noticed something different about her. There was Edwin Jones at his desk, bending his thin nose over a book. Cathy put her hand down on the page.

"What would you like to be when you grow up, Edwin?"

Edwin looked at her hand and then looked up at her. Edwin Jones always took a long time before he spoke.

"A pirate," he said finally.

Katie stared at the boy. With his pale yellow hair and thin nose he looked more like a baby chick than a pirate.

"A pirate!" She laughed. "That's silly. Nobody can be a pirate any more."

She flounced her skirts as she turned, calling, "Priscilla, did you hear what—" Then she noticed that Edwin's face was pink as he bent over his book again. Katie closed her mouth. And now she remembered something. Edwin hadn't picked potatoes off of her and laughed at her when the other boys did. Katie John came back to his desk.

"I'm sorry," she said. "That was dumb of me to laugh. I guess you can be a pirate if you want to."

Edwin fingered the page of his book. "No, I can't. I'll probably be just any old thing." He looked at her and saw she wasn't laughing. "But you asked what I'd *like* to be, and what I'd *like* to be is a pirate."

Katie understood. "I know. I suppose I'll be a housewife when I grow up, but it's more fun to think I'll be a circus acrobat. Just the same, Edwin Jones, I bet you do something exciting when you grow up."

Edwin turned pink again. But this time he didn't look miserable.

Oh, dear, she'd forgotten all about being Cathy, talking about being a circus acrobat, of all things. She sighed as she went back to her desk. It was hard being a lady.

After school Cathy-Katie and Sue walked toward Main Street to buy valentines at the dime store. Behind them Cathy saw Howard and some of the other boys coming along. She felt a little thrill of excitement. Were they going downtown to buy valentines, too? Would they buy valentines for her? They saw her. She tucked a little demure smile in at the corners of her mouth and pretended not to see them.

"Don't look," she whispered to Sue.

"Hey, Katie," Howard hollered. "Got any potatoes today?"

The corners of her mouth turned sour. The boys came whooping up behind the girls, and the next thing they were sprinkling sleety snow over Katie John.

"Oh, goody, here's Hot-Potato Katie," Pete squealed. "She's covered with potato."

The boys began the same old business of pretending to eat potato off of Katie John, picking at the snow. Katie saw red.

"All right for you guys," she yelled. "I've had just about enough of this potato business!"

She snatched up a fistful of icy snow packed in a wicked hard ball and heaved it at Howard.

"Snowball fight!" the boys shouted happily. They grabbed up snow.

"I'll hot potato you," Katie cried, shoving slushy snow down Howard's neck.

A snowball hit her on the shoulder. Howard tried to

hold her to wash her face in the snow, and Pete and Sammy ran up to help. Sue was off at the side, screaming "Cathy! Cathy!"

Katie John heard her. She stopped struggling with the boys—and got a mouthful of snow. She spit it out. Heavens above, she wasn't being Cathy. There was her green hair ribbon being trampled in the slush under Sammy's feet. Some lady! But Howard was off guard now. What a chance! She slammed big handfuls of snow square in his face. There, she'd fixed him!

Katie pulled away from the boys and ran, shouting for Sue to come on. Fiddlesticks. She could never be Priscilla Simmons. She might just as well be herself. More fun that way, anyway.

"Never mind calling me Cathy," she told Sue, breathless and laughing.

At the dime store, though, she had a sudden thought. "What about the boys? Do we give valentines to the boys?"

"Oh, don't worry about that," Sue said. "The girls

always give penny valentines to all the boys. Of course, if you have someone special, you give a nicer one to him. I'm going to get a dime one for Bob."

"Well, I haven't got anyone special," Katie declared.

Just the same, she searched carefully in the penny valentines for a pirate one for Edwin Jones.

Friday, when valentine time came, Katie John told herself she wouldn't get any valentines from boys and she didn't care. Nevertheless, she sat as tensely as the rest of the girls. Miss Howell began reading off the names. Priscilla Simmons' was the first. That figured. Katie watched her walk modestly up the aisle.

Katie had wondered whether to send valentines to Priscilla and some of her friends. She'd decided to play it safe and send penny valentines to everyone in the room, except for a lovely lavender one for Miss Howell and an especially pretty double-heart one for Sue.

"Katie John," Miss Howell was calling.

Katie's heart gave a sudden thump. She went up to Miss Howell's desk, and Miss Howell handed her several of the penny-sized valentines, plus a bigger one. At her desk Katie bent her head low because she could feel her face burning as she opened the envelopes. The big one contained a pretty frilly heart from Sue. The little ones were from girls. She let out a breath. Were these all she'd get? No, the other children were going back and forth to Miss Howell's desk several times, especially Priscilla.

"More for Katie John," Miss Howell called.

Katie's hands felt very light and prickly as she went back up the aisle. Don't be dumb, she told herself. You know you won't get any from boys.

Miss Howell was trying to get the passing out over with, and she'd sorted a handful of envelopes for Katie.

"That's all of them for you," she said, smiling.

There was another big one in the stack. Katie tried not to notice it, because it made her heart pound. She saved it for last.

She opened one of the small envelopes. But this wasn't a regular penny valentine. It was a folded sheet of plain paper. She spread it out. Colored on it with brown crayon was a fat potato, with stick arms and legs and a girl head with bangs. Underneath was written: "BE MY BAKED POTATO." It was signed "Howard."

Katie stared at the awful thing. Then she tore at the other envelopes. Sure enough, except for one penny valentine from a girl, they were all from boys. And they all had colored potato girls and said the same thing, "BE MY BAKED POTATO."

Comic valentines! Katie John didn't know whether to laugh or to cry. At last she looked up and saw Howard and the other boys watching her. Oh, all right, she'd be a good sport. She grinned and held her nose, and the boys laughed.

There remained the big envelope. Katie opened it slowly. Inside was a beautiful pink satin heart with lace edges. She sucked in her breath and turned the card over. No name was signed. Who—?

Katie stared around the room. And saw Edwin Jones just looking away, the tips of his ears bright pink, as pink as the satin heart. So!

Katie John let out her breath. There was a silly prickling around her eyeballs, and she blinked her eyes quickly. No one gave satin hearts to tomboys. With one finger she touched the softness of the heart. Then very carefully she slid the card back into its envelope. She had a feeling that this was one valentine she'd keep for a long, long time.

At War with the Renters

Katie John lay in bed with her eyes open. Through the dark she could see the green luminous dial of the clock on her bedstand. Twenty minutes to eleven. No point in trying to go to sleep now. Mr. Watkins would be coming downstairs any minute.

She couldn't sleep, anyway. It had been a grubbly day, a stupid, all-round grubbly day, from beginning to end. She'd missed seven words on the spelling test. And she'd had to stay in at recess for whispering. Then when she'd come home from school, Mother and Dad had been very quiet and gloomy. The publisher didn't want to buy Dad's book about the newspaper business. After all Dad's work— "No, thank you." Why, he'd written on it for a year. Of course Dad said he'd try another publisher, but his face wasn't hopeful. At first Katie had been surprised. She hadn't realized that sometimes books didn't get published, even after people went to all the work of writing them. But now she felt like crying. Dad had looked so discouraged.

Katie flopped her hot pillow over. Besides, they'd been counting on the book money. Now what would they do? The rent money was barely enough to live on. She knew, for she'd heard Mother and Dad talking in low, worried voices sometimes.

And that was another grubbly thing. The renters. Some of them were getting to be such nuisances. Yes, there. There came Mr. Watkins. Ta-ump, ta-ump, ta-ump. He was coming down the stairs from the third floor, off for his night watchman's job at the flour mill. Mr. Watkins was a heavy man, and he didn't run down the stairs lightly. No, each foot came down on each step slowly and exactly, one at a time, ta-ump, ta-ump, ta-ump, in the silent house.

Mother and Dad used to go to bed at ten o'clock, but now they didn't try to sleep until after Mr. Watkins left each night. For just as they were going to sleep in their second-floor bedroom, Mr. Watkins was getting up, bumping around in his room above, fixing something to eat, getting ready for work. Now the Tuckers read in bed until the ta-umps had gone down the stairs.

Usually Katie John was asleep when Mr. Watkins left for work, but his journey down the house often woke her. She knew just how many steps there were in each flight of stairs. Ta-ump, seventeen, ta-ump, eighteen. There, he'd reached the second floor. Along the hall, twenty-one more ta-umps to the first floor. She counted along with him— Oh, hurry up. Ta-ump, nineteen, ta-ump, twenty—long silence, waiting, waiting. For weeks Katie had wondered what on earth was going on before

he took that last step down. At last she'd realized that
he was looking on the newel post for letters. That was
where Mother put the renters' mail. Ta-ump, twenty-
one! And slam! went the front door, shaking the
house.

Katie sighed and her body relaxed. Now she could
sleep. It was silly, of course, to be mad at somebody just
because you don't like the way he walks down the stairs.
But it was no fun being waked up almost every night . . .
Well, go to sleep . . . What a sad mess of renters they
had living in their house, though. Oh, Mr. Watkins was
probably all right, other than his clumping. He always
smiled politely. And of course Miss Howell and her sister, Miss Julia, were perfect. Mr. Peters, the riverman,
was all right, too. He kept his basement apartment neat,
so that Katie and her mother never had to clean his rooms,
only wash his sheets and towels each week. Buster was
a pest, but at least he hadn't fallen in any water this
winter. Probably because the river was frozen over. He
went to swimming classes at the YMCA two afternoons a
week, and that seemed to satisfy him—and keep him out
of Katie's way for a while.

So she shouldn't really say *all* the renters were a mess.
But some of them! The tourists, for instance, that sometimes rented the empty third-floor rooms. Here one night,
gone the next day, leaving a cluttered room to clean up
and sheets to wash, all for one night's rent. One traveling
salesman stayed for a week, but plopped himself down in

the Tuckers' parlor every night, just as if it was a hotel lobby.

And then there was Mr. Peabody. He was quiet enough, but he never paid his rent. Every time Dad asked him for it, Mr. Peabody had some long, hard-luck story, and once he even tried to borrow money from Dad.

Go to sleep. Gladys and Pearl were the worst renters, though. They were always pestering Dad to fix something in their room. And they were awful grouches, always complaining to Katie that she didn't bring them enough wood for their fireplace. At night, though, they were cheery enough when they had their girl friends over. Then it was cackle and shriek—ha-ha! They had the room above Katie's, and she'd never known middle-aged women could be so noisy. Even when they weren't having a party their radio whined on and on with those awful hill-billy songs that all sounded alike.

Now she just must go to sleep. It was after eleven— Oh, no! A key was rattling in the front-door lock. Think of the devil—here came Gladys and Pearl. The front hall light clicked on, and the women clacked up the stairs talking loud as broad daylight about the movie they'd just seen. They don't care that the house was all quiet and dark and put to bed, Katie thought. Now they were tromping around above her. Yep. There went the radio. "Ah had the sweetest dream," a man sang through his nose.

"Oh—oh, blast!" She kicked at her covers. Now she'd

never get to sleep. She pulled her pillow over her head. But the nose-singing came through the feathers— "Mah dream was pink and purple—"

Tomorrow was Saturday. Gladys and Pearl didn't have to work tomorrow at the egg factory. They might stay up half the night. But *she* had to work. How could she help with all the Saturday housecleaning, if she didn't get any sleep at all?

Katie swung her feet out of bed. "I'm just going to tell them!"

She padded along the hall to the stairs. She could see quite well, for the women had left the hall light on as usual. Without a sound she ran up the stairs, through the door to the back wing of the house, and knocked on the women's door. Gladys opened it. She was wearing a wrapper and had her stringy hair half up in curlers. Pearl was sitting by the radio, and the room was full of cowboy music.

"Would you mind turning off your radio?" Katie asked, politely enough. "It's keeping me awake."

Gladys looked at her, no friendliness in her face, no nothing, just blank.

"Okay, kid, pretty soon," she said. She shut the door in Katie's face.

Oh! Katie John ran back downstairs, turned off the hall light, and climbed into bed. Her clock said eleven-fifteen. She closed her eyes. The radio went right on, "Yew are the sunrise, and mah storm-clouds, too."

Great-Aunt Emily would turn over in her grave if she knew. That was her private sitting room that Gladys and Pearl and the hillbillies were living in. Katie had had such fun last summer exploring Aunt Emily's desk up there, looking at her keepsakes, learning to know what Aunt Emily had been like as a girl, even though Katie never met Aunt Emily before she died as an old, old lady. She'd learned to love her Great-Aunt Emily Clark in that room up there. And now look. Wet stockings hanging from the lamp, pink plaster dolls on Aunt Emily's desk, and two mean women living there.

"Yew send a shower—" They weren't going to turn off that radio until they got good and ready, Katie realized.

"It's not fair. This is our house, not theirs."

Her eyes felt gravelly from being awake and wanting to be asleep.

I'd like to march up there and throw that radio out the window.

If the electricity went off in the house, that would shut off that noise fast enough. Maybe—

Katie John got out of bed and put on her robe and slippers. She went down to the basement, feeling her way in the dark. In the laundry room she turned on a light. On the wall was the bank of fuse boxes for the big house. Katie studied them. They were labeled with cards in Aunt Emily's neat writing. "Lights, front, first floor.

Wall sockets, front, first floor." She read along. Ah, here. "Wall sockets, rear, second floor."

Katie reached up and unscrewed the round fuse just a little. Just enough to disconnect things but leave the fuse in the box. Now! She turned off the basement light, tiptoed up the cellar steps to the hall, and listened. Not a sound from the radio.

She hurried back to bed. Above she could hear Gladys and Pearl fretting about the radio.

"Try another station."

"Must be a tube burned out."

"Oh, well, let's go to bed."

Katie John grinned and closed her eyes.

She had hoped she'd silenced the radio forever. The next morning, however, Pearl tried to plug in their electric toaster, and it wouldn't work either. When the women could get neither their morning toast nor their morning music they complained to Mr. Tucker. Katie was in the laundry room starting the first load of renters' sheets in the washing machine when Dad looked at the fuse boxes to see if a fuse had burned out.

"Why, the fuse is unscrewed," Dad said. "Now how could that happen?"

"Maybe we had a little earthquake in the night and it jarred loose," Katie said, trying to keep her voice straight.

Dad looked at her suspiciously, but she made herself

very busy at working the cantankerous wringer on the old washing machine.

Gladys and Pearl had won, though. When Katie John went back upstairs, the guitar music was wailing the same as ever.

Muttering to herself, Katie stomped up the steps to Mr. Peabody's room, dragging the broom after her. Mother was scrubbing the third-floor bathroom.

"What?" Mother asked, as Katie muttered past.

"Oh, nothing," Katie grunted.

Mr. Peabody was away at work. What a clutter his room was. Detective magazines scattered on the window seat, clothes thrown on the chairs. Katie started to pull the sheets off the unmade bed, then stopped. Mr. Peabody never paid his rent. Why should he get clean sheets? She made up the bed with the old sheets still on it. Then she swept all his dirty socks into the closet and whisked briefly at the floor with her broom. Never mind the corners.

"That's all the cleaning you get till you pay the rent," she told the room.

She banged Mr. Peabody's door shut after her and pushed up her bangs. Maybe that would teach him a lesson. She felt hateful, but she didn't care. It was their house, and the renters didn't have any right to make such awful pests of themselves. It was about time somebody made the renters behave.

Now to sweep down the stairs—all the dirt the renters

tracked in—and hang out the sheets. Then she could go play with Sue. Katie had her pile of dirt almost down to the first floor when Mr. Watkins came in the front door. He was carrying his black lunch pail and he looked tired. Well, she was tired, too, from practically no sleep last night. He'd started it all. She spiked up her bangs again and faced him squarely.

"Mr. Watkins," she began.

"Good morning, Miss Katie." His thick face smiled politely.

"Mr. Watkins," she went on, "we try to be quiet in the afternoon and evening so you can sleep, don't we?"

"Yes . . . ?"

"Well, I know you don't realize it, but you wake us up every night when you go to work. You walk so loud when you go downstairs. Would you please try to be more quiet?"

Mr. Watkins quit smiling. He looked down at his large feet.

"Yes, of course. I didn't know. Yes, I'll be more quiet."

He tiptoed up the stairs, the steps creaking under his weight. Katie jabbed her broom at the dirt on the steps.

I suppose now I've hurt his feelings, she thought angrily. But—well—a person has to stand up for her rights.

Somehow today was turning out to be just as grubbly as yesterday.

When she finally got down to Sue's house, Sue was

gone. Her big sister, Janet, said Sue was shopping with her mother. Then in the afternoon Katie had to baby-sit Buster because Mr. Peters was gone somewhere. It was too cold and windy for Buster to play outside, and he didn't want to play any nice indoor games. All he wanted was for Katie John to read *Three Little Pigs* to him—that baby story. She'd read it to him so many times this winter she hoped she'd never see another pig in her life. At last she got Buster settled at building with plastic bricks and was about to curl up in the big chair with a good book when Mother came into the parlor.

"Katie John, did you forget to change Mr. Peabody's sheets?"

"No— I didn't on purpose."

"And you didn't clean his room very well, either."

"Mother, he doesn't deserve to have his room cleaned. He never pays his rent."

Katie was conscious of Mother's eyes on her, and she looked down, picking at her fingernails.

"Katie John, it's not a little girl's place to reform grownups. Katie, is it?"

She wouldn't look up. "No. But I don't like—"

"I know. You don't like certain things that people do, so you try to change them. But there are some things you can't change. You simply have to accept them."

Katie continued to push the skin back from her nails. Mother stood across the room from her. It was as if they were on opposite sides of a wall.

At last Mother said, "Very well. Please change the sheets on Mr. Peabody's bed now."

Katie John got up and walked out of the room without looking at Mother. She took clean sheets from the linen chest in the back hall and climbed up to the third floor. She pulled the dirty sheets off the bed and began to re-make it.

I don't care. It isn't fair.

And then on the way back downstairs Pearl had to stick her head out of her door.

"Katie John, we're all out of firewood. I told you you didn't bring enough the last time."

Katie looked at Pearl's freckled face and said, "Okay. Pretty soon." Just the way Gladys had said it about the radio.

"What do you mean, pretty soon? You get that wood right now, young lady, or I'll tell your ma!"

Katie John stalked past Pearl and took her own sweet time going down the stairs until she was out of the woman's sight. Then she raced on down to the basement, the wooden cellar stairs thundering under her feet. She dumped Mr. Peabody's sheets in a laundry tub and swiped hot tears off her cheeks. She began throwing wood into a cardboard box.

I just hate her. I hate all of them. I'm just a servant to a bunch of nasty renters. All the time answering the phone for them and washing their sheets and dragging wood upstairs for their fireplaces. And they're going to go right on being mean, and there isn't anything I can do about it.

Whack, she threw the wood in the box. There was a great lump in her throat that she couldn't swallow. She stared at the wood.

Well, I will do something. I'll fix them.

She grabbed up four bricks from a pile near the firewood and put them in the box. Panting, she ran upstairs with her load. At Pearl's door she dumped the box of wood but took the bricks with her. On up to the top of the house she stormed.

In the third floor a last short flight of steps led up to a trap door in the roof. Katie unfastened the catch and pushed at the door, arms over her head in the cramped space under the roof. Ugh—it was heavy. But Katie heaved fiercely, and the door lifted sideways on its hinges. She took the bricks from the stairs and stepped out onto the flat roof.

It was almost dark now, and the wind struck her, whipping her blouse, a wild wind, as wild as she felt. She ran across the roof to two brick chimneys rising chest high from the roof. Across the blackened openings of each chimney she placed two bricks. There! Now let those nasty renters try lighting a fire in their fireplaces. They'd get a roomful of smoke. She'd plugged up their chimneys. One served Mr. Peabody's and Mr. Watkins' rooms, and the other led to the fireplaces in Pearl's room and in Katie's. And she'd just do without a fire. It was worth it!

Whump, something thumped on the roof. The door. The wind had blown the trap door shut! Katie ran over to it, pulled at the edges, tried to lift it.

It wouldn't move.

But that couldn't be. She had to get down off the roof.

She pulled desperately. The door wouldn't budge. The latch must have caught when it slammed shut.

Katie John stood up and looked around. There was no other way down from the roof. None of the treetops, lashing in the wind, were close enough to the roof. She was all alone on top of the house, and no one even knew she was here. And it was cold, bitterly cold. She hadn't thought of getting a coat. Far below lay the river, white and still with ice. Katie hugged her arms across her chest and looked out through the dusk over the town. Last summer, when she'd come up here with Dad, the top of Barton's Bluff had been bushy green with leaves, only the church steeple sticking above. Now the trees were bare, and she could see all the warm lights of houses blinking on. Everyone was home safe for the night but her. She was shut out of her own house.

Carefully Katie stepped as near to the edge of the roof as she dared. The wind might blow her off, or she might slip . . . "Help!" she called down to the street, but the street was empty. "Up here!" The wind swallowed her voice.

Oh, the door *must* open. She ran back and tugged

with cold fingers. No good. It was as if the door had grown fast to the roof.

Her parents wouldn't even know where to look for her. She might have to stay up here all night. She'd freeze.

If only she could make someone hear her.

"Oh, help!" she cried, pounding on the door with her fists.

But of course there was no one in the third floor now to hear her. Wait—yes, there was. Mr. Watkins should be sleeping in his room.

Katie John ran to a chimney and got a brick. This part should be right over his room. She pounded the brick on the roof as hard as she could and shouted down the chimney: "Help! Mr. Watkins! Help!" He ought to hear. Last summer, when rain drummed on the flat roof, it had sounded loud as a hailstorm. But she couldn't hear a sound from below. Mr. Watkins slept so soundly.

She beat the roof with the brick, crying over and over, "Help! Mr. Watkins!" It was black dark now, and frosty stars quivered far above. Maybe if he heard he wouldn't know what to think. She ran to the trap door and pounded on it.

It was lifting! And there was Mr. Watkins' heavy face.

"Oh, Mr. Watkins! Oh, thank goodness!"

Holding the door up, he stared at her as if he could hardly understand what he was seeing.

"Miss Katie! What are you doing up there?"

"I—" A burning blush rushed over her face. She looked at him, unable to speak.

Mr. Watkins smiled. "Never mind. Come on down."

"Wait." She ran back to the chimneys and got the other three bricks. Then she climbed down onto the steps while Mr. Watkins held the door.

Standing in the hall cradling the bricks in her arms, she tried. "I'm so glad you—I mean I'm sorry I woke you up, but— Oh, Mr. Watkins, thank you! And I'm sorry for what I said this morning."

"Now, now." He kept patting her shoulder. "It's all right. You better go downstairs and get warm."

That night Katie John lay awake in bed for a long time. The house was quiet. Still, she couldn't sleep. She wished she could tell Mr. Watkins to go ahead and clump on the stairs all he wanted. But of course, she couldn't. He already realized, and anything she said now would only make him more self-conscious.

She remembered something that happened when she was a little girl. A doctor had come to visit her when she had the measles, and while he was out of her room briefly she'd hopped out of bed and poked around in his black satchel. In the process she'd dropped his thermometer on the floor. It had broken, and its blobs of mercury had run out on the carpet. In a panic she'd tried to pick up the mercury, put it back somehow. But no matter how she tried, the silvery bubbles of mercury slipped away from her fingers. She couldn't put them back.

At last Katie heard a creaking on the stairs. Mr. Watkins was tiptoeing down the stairs. There was a silence. He must be putting on his shoes. Then the front door closed softly.

Katie John's pillow was wet before she slept.

Heavenly Spot

Then Heavenly Spot came into Katie John's life.

It was the morning of her eleventh birthday, and she was full of the strangeness of being eleven all of a sudden. Eleven sounded so much older than ten, so grown up and solemn. She wasn't sure she knew how to be eleven. She'd asked for a pretty jumper and a frilly blouse, just in case she ever wanted special clothes.

Her best present so far, however, had been the bicycle. True, it was a secondhand bike. Money was still scarce at the Tuckers' house. Katie didn't care. It was newly painted blue, it had two wheels, and it would take her places. Ever since last summer she'd been wanting a bike to explore the countryside around Barton's Bluff.

Before Katie John could try out the bicycle, Buster came upstairs, his eyes sparkling with a secret.

"Hap' birthday," he said. "Dad says come down to our place for a minute."

More birthday excitement. Katie John followed Buster down the basement steps, and Mr. Peters met them at the apartment door.

"Dog," he said. "Your folks said it was all right. Want him?"

"A dog!"

She saw him then, snuffling at something under the table, his long brown ears flopping forward. Immediately Katie John knew that here was the dearest, finest, smartest dog in the whole wide world. And he was made just for her. He was some kind of small, sturdy hound, not much past puppyhood. His back was black, his head, tail, and legs were a smooth golden brown, and at the end of his long brown tail was a shining white spot. The dog looked up at Katie John and grinned out a moist pink tongue.

"Oh, Mr. Peters!" Katie cried. "He's beautiful!"

"Well." Mr. Peters stuck his hands in his pockets, embarrassed. "Friend of mine was giving away dogs. This'n ain't purebred. Got some beagle in him, I guess. Mostly just a Missouri houn' dog."

"But he *is* beautiful," Katie insisted. She knelt by the dog and smoothed back his ears, smiling into his eyes. "See how his colors follow the shape of his body just so? And that spot on his tail. Such a clean white. As if God had drawn him all perfectly, and when He came to the end, He said, 'There!' and dotted the tip of the tail. And His finger made a shining spot. Oh, Mr. Peters, I'm going to call this dog Heavenly Spot!"

Mr. Peters' button eyes were startled. He shook his

head doubtfully. "I never heard no Missouri houn' dog called that before."

"Some name," Buster said, disgusted.

Katie didn't want to offend Mr. Peters after he'd given her such a perfectly wonderful birthday dog.

"All right," she agreed, "I'll call him Spot, for short."

Mr. Peters looked relieved, and Buster tousled the dog's head, saying, "Yeah, good old Spot." But Katie John thought to herself, I'll call you Spot, but I'll think of you as Heavenly Spot.

She wanted to throw her arms around Mr. Peters and kiss him for giving her such a dear dog. But the little riverman's eyes grew startled again when she turned to him, so she grabbed his hand instead and shook it hard.

"Thank you, Mr. Peters!" she said. "Thank you very, very much!"

Katie John led Heavenly Spot out into the basement to be alone with him. She knelt on the brick floor and took his head in her hands. When the dog's tongue slid out to lick her hands, she laughed, then looked into his eyes seriously.

"Spot, I am your master," she told him. "You are my dog."

The hound swished his tail agreeably on the bricks.

Katie John jumped up. "Now come on, Spot." She wanted to show him to her folks.

Spot jumped up, too, but he headed in the opposite

direction. Off toward the coal cellar he ran, nose to the floor, brown tail sticking straight up like an exclamation mark, white spot shining like a signal: Heavenly Spot was trailing something.

Oh, fiddle. He must have smelled a mouse. That's right, hounds were good at following smells. Well, he could track down his mouse later.

"Here, Spot! Come on!"

Spot must not know his name. Or the smell was awfully juicy.

"Spot! Come *here!*"

At last Katie had to pick him up and carry him upstairs. Spot was still puppy enough to enjoy being carried. He tucked his nose against her neck.

"Silly dog," she scolded him lovingly. "Don't you know I'm your master now? You must come when I call."

She'd have to call him by name a lot so he'd learn his name—and to come. Katie John soon discovered there was much more for a dog master to do. She had to feed him—messy job, mixing his food. She had to brush him. She had to teach him to ask to go outdoors—and she had to clean up the puddles. And when she took him for a walk to show him off to Sue and the neighborhood, she had to keep chasing after him when he ran away, trailing snowbirds and sparrows.

By the end of her eleventh birthday the new dog master was happy and tired from taking care of her pet. As she climbed into bed she muttered suspiciously, "I don't think he knows yet who's supposed to be master." She smiled, turning her cheek to the pillow. "He'll learn, though." The dear dog. Happy flopping ears and waving white spot blurred into a dream. The dream dog was trailing elephant footprints through an autumn woods. Suddenly he pointed his nose to a huge yellow moon and howled. Ow-oooo-ooo. And the moon fell down with an awful clatter.

Katie John sat straight up in her bed. What? The howl went on outside her window. The clatter continued on her ceiling. Gladys and Pearl were pounding their floor above Katie. And the howl— Oh, dear, Heavenly Spot must be waking them up with his howling. She had made a nice bed for him in the brick barn behind the house, but the poor dog must be lonesome and cold.

She opened her window and called out, "Spot! Be quiet! Hush up!"

Katie crawled back into her warm bed. But Heavenly Spot was a true Missouri hound dog, and if his first business was trailing, his next-best business was howling. OW-OOOOOO, he told the world in a round tone that went up and down the scale. The banging on the ceiling began again.

The dog master threw back her covers. "Oh, all right!" She stuck her feet into slippers and made a quick trip out into the cold night. Then she curled back into her bed, with Heavenly Spot warm on her feet.

Next morning, though, Dad told Katie John she'd

only rewarded Spot for howling by bringing him into the house. If he howled at night again, she was to go out with a rolled-up newspaper and swat the ground beside him, sternly saying *no!* Which Katie did, for many nights afterward, until Spot finally got the idea. The renters were very unhappy with it all.

Katie didn't care. Heavenly Spot was worth any amount of trouble. And what a wonderful combination her birthday presents were proving to be—a bike for exploring the country roads and a dog to run alongside. Whenever the March weather permitted, Katie John rode out to the woods and pastures to see the pussy willows putting out silvery knobs and the brooks having their busy season, rushing full with melting snow.

Sometimes Sue rode with her, but there was one place Katie John preferred to visit alone, with only her dog for company. It was a little overgrown cemetery back in the trees on a bluff above the river. No one had been buried there since 1902, according to the dates on the gravestones. Katie liked to study the mossy markers while the hound pup nosed around in the woods after rabbit smell.

"Pioneers, Oh, Pioneers," said one gray stone. That person had been born 'way back in 1829. In another spot Samuel Bentley had three wives buried around him. And here were a father and son who'd died the same day. Maybe a bear had got them. The little cemetery was a good spot for thinking, too—or not thinking, as she sat on a stone and looked down at the river. She'd found the graveyard one day when she'd been mad about something, and by the time she'd left, she'd forgotten all about her mad.

Yes, it looked as though she had a perfect spring ahead of her, with a bike and a dog. If only that hound dog would quit trailing things. Of course, it was all right for him to trail things out in the country, but he kept trailing smells in town, too. And there lay trouble.

Unfortunately, many of the smell trails seemed to lead to Miss Crackenberry's garden next door. Last summer Katie John had fretted because the old lady's snappy little dog, Prince, kept digging in Aunt Emily's vegetables. Now it was a very embarrassing situation, with Miss Crackenberry telephoning almost every day for Katie to come after her dog. The last time Katie John hauled her dog home, Miss Crackenberry warned her, "Mark my words, that dog will end up in the gas box."

That had frightened Katie. The gas box was the place at the police station where wandering dogs were put to sleep forever. She didn't know what the box looked like, or where it was located in the police station. But once, when she was passing the little garden around the police station, she heard a dog howling. And then he stopped. It made her shudder and wonder.

Most of all, though, Heavenly Spot trailed Katie. She'd started right away to teach him not to follow her to school. "Stay!" she'd say sternly, pointing to the ground. Being quite a smart dog, Heavenly Spot would stay. All the way down the block Katie could look back and see Spot's head poked out the front gate, watching her. But often as not, when Katie came out of school at mid-morning recess, there would be her hound dog, full of bounce and looking for praise for being so clever as to trail her. He was always so proud and delighted to see her, Katie usually couldn't bring herself to scold him.

There came a day when she wished she'd tried harder to break Spot's trailing habits. When she came home from school, the dog was gone, and Mother said he must be out following a smell. By dark he still hadn't come home. Katie worried through her supper. Maybe he'd roamed too far this time. Maybe the dogcatcher had picked him up. Maybe—

"I'm going to the dog pound at the police station," she told her parents.

She flung on her coat and hurried down the dark, windy street. The police station was only a few blocks away. It was a neat little building set in a garden with paths and benches and a white stone wishing well. The well was artificial, though. Katie and Sue had looked in it before, and there was no water in it, only floor boards. In the back of the police station were the kennels where stray dogs were kept. Katie could hear dogs barking, but none of the yips sounded like Heavenly Spot's voice.

A young policeman with a square face sat behind a desk.

"Have you killed any dogs today?" Katie asked.

If the policeman was surprised to see a girl blow through the door with such a question, he didn't show it.

"No."

Well, that was a relief!

"My dog is lost. I wonder if he's here."

She began to describe Spot, and the policeman was shaking his head when a dog ran in the door she'd left open behind her. Snuffling and licking and so glad to see her—it was Heavenly Spot.

"Oh, you worrisome dog!" Katie cried, hugging him. "I was so afraid you were in the gas box!"

The policeman said he'd never seen Spot before, so the dog must have trailed her here.

"Please call me if the dogcatcher ever does pick up Spot," Katie John begged, and the policeman promised.

The very next Sunday, however, Heavenly Spot finally reached the gas box.

The trouble began when Katie was sitting in the choir stalls at St. John's Church. Some time ago Sue had persuaded her to join the children's choir, even though Katie's voice was on the croaky side. Every Sunday Katie John put on the black choir robes and sang at the nine-thirty family service. Sometimes her parents attended that service, but this Sunday they planned to come to the later service.

Katie was just settling back onto the choir bench after kneeling during prayers when she heard a sound that didn't belong in church, a snicker somewhere in the back. She looked to see who was so naughty. Goodness! Was she dreaming? Trotting up the center aisle, nose to the carpet, long tail high, white spot gleaming at the tip— Heavenly Spot. Right to the choir stalls he came. He looked up, saw Katie, and sat down, grinning at her.

Oh, dear. He was real.

Now more people were snickering. Katie John wanted to throw her choir robes over her head and die right there.

"Would someone please put the dog out?" the minister asked.

A boy in the front pew jumped up. He snapped his fingers at the dog, but Heavenly Spot kept right on panting happily with his eyes on Katie. The boy picked him up and carried him out.

Katie scrooched down in her seat and stared at her hymnal. But she knew her face was flaming and that everyone could see her, for she was sitting at the end of the stall nearest the congregation. Oh, Spot, how could you! Thank goodness, the minister was announcing a song. People would look at their hymnbooks and forget about her. "Fling out the banner, let it float," Katie tried to sing.

But, oh, dear goodness, here came Spot again! It was a warm day for March, and the outside door was open. If that boy had thought the inner swinging doors would stop a determined dog, he didn't know Heavenly Spot.

Tail spot held like a banner, he ran up to the choir

stalls and sat down again. Maybe the singing hurt his
ears, or maybe he was just sociable. Anyway, Heavenly
Spot pointed his nose to the roof and howled. Howled a
mournful Missouri hound-dog howl to the tune of "Fling
out the Banner."

There was only one thing to do. Katie John leaned
down from the stall, grabbed her dog's front legs, and
dragged him up. Holding him in her arms, she pushed
past the row of choir children and escaped through the
little back door behind the choir loft.

Stairs led down under the organ pipes. Katie stumbled
down the steps, carrying the dog. Oh, the disgrace! The
pipes throbbed mightily, here so close, and Heavenly Spot
howled in protest.

"Bad dog!" Katie spanked his bottom. "Bad dog!"

Heavenly Spot yipped in surprise. Katie just hoped the organ was covering their noise.

She reached the basement. Now what to do? If she put Spot out, he'd come right back in again. She could stay down here with him until church was over. But he might howl again. No, she'd just have to take him home. The organ pealed above, and the hound pointed his nose. Katie clapped her hand over his mouth. She'd have to get him out of here right away.

Lugging the heavy dog, she hurried to the basement stairs that led up to a side door on the sidewalk. She ran out into the March sunshine that was melting remains of slush in the street. Along the sidewalk she ran holding Spot until she was well away from the church. Then she put him down and spanked him again.

"Bad dog!"

Heavenly Spot whimpered and his white spot drooped to the sidewalk. But Katie John hardened her heart.

"Now come on." She ran toward home, with Spot galloping after her, full of spirits again.

It felt strange to be out here on the nearly-empty streets while the church service went on without her. Then she saw some people in a car staring at her, and she slowed to a walk. Oh, for heavens' sake. She hadn't thought how she must look, tearing down the street in her long black choir robe and round black cap. In church the robes looked just right, the proper things to wear. Out here on the street they were so out of place she might as well be wearing a Zulu outfit. She might as well be running down the street naked. She wished she were invisible. She wished she could just shrivel down to the sidewalk.

"Oh, you dog!"

Now it seemed as if there were people everywhere—a woman looking out her window, more cars passing, children laughing and pointing. Katie rounded the corner by the police station. Only three more blocks to home.

But who was that tiny figure at the end of the block? Miss Crackenberry! Oh, wouldn't you know! Here came Miss Crackenberry, nice and early for the eleven-o'clock service. Black straw hat set squarely on her head, long black skirt almost brushing the sidewalk, the little old woman came marching along. She hadn't seen Katie yet. She was looking down at her hands, smoothing her black gloves.

Katie John stood in a panic. She just couldn't let Miss Crackenberry see her like this. The old lady would never stop talking about it and smiling her thin, satisfied smile. Hide. Where could she hide?

She grabbed up Heavenly Spot, the startled dog struggling against her arms. Run into the police station? No, there in the garden. The little white stone wishing well. She could hide there.

Katie dashed into the garden, hoping Miss Crackenberry was nearsighted and hadn't seen this far. Over the side of the well she scrambled and crouched down on the boards. Heavenly Spot didn't like it here, but she held him down. She could hear Miss Crackenberry's heels on the sidewalk, cr-t, cr-t, cr-t. Go on by, Katie willed. Go right on by.

Heavenly Spot must have developed a taste for howling this morning, however, for he chose this moment to lift his nose and utter a choice tone. O-o-w-w!

Cr-t! The heels stopped. Katie clamped the dog's jaws shut with both hands and stopped breathing. All was silence in the well, except for Spot's faint snuffling as he tried to get his jaws loose.

Scr-tch scr-tch, the heels were coming along the gravel path in the garden. Katie John closed her eyes. But no, the heels went on past to the police station. No sound. Then voices coming back out of the station.

Miss Crackenberry's, saying "—shame to kill dogs on the Sabbath."

And a man's rumble, saying, "Madam, you are mistaken. We aren't."

"But I heard a dog howling in the gas box," Miss Crackenberry insisted.

Katie's eyes snapped open in horror. Was *this* the gas box? Oh, it couldn't be. She glanced at the walls and the open air above. Then she saw the handle on the boards under her. The floor must lift up, a trap door. And underneath— No wonder Heavenly Spot howled in this place!

"Look if you like," the policeman was saying.

"No, I don't want to look in the nasty place," the old lady replied.

"Then I'll check."

Katie's hand flew to her mouth. She raised her head, and there was the policeman with the square face looking down at her. Katie made a shushing gesture with her finger to her lips, her eyes begging him. He looked at the scene in the gas-box well, the crouching girl in her black choir robes with a struggling dog squashed under her. And his face didn't change expression. Maybe he'd seen so many strange sights in his police work that nothing startled him.

At any rate, he straightened and said to Miss Cracken-berry, "No, ma'am, no dogs being killed today."

"Well, if you say so—"

Scr-tch scr-tch, the heels went away.

When the sound of the heels was completely gone, Katie John let out a gusty breath and let go of Heavenly Spot's jaws. As he gratefully licked his nose, she told him, "Heavenly Spot, you've been to the gas box and lived to tell the tale."

She lifted him over the side of the well onto the ground. The policeman was still standing by the well, his face not quite so square, now that the corners of his mouth kept trying to turn up.

"This dog seems to cause you quite a bit of trouble," he said.

"Yes, the pesky thing!"

"Want us to take him off your hands? We could find another home for him."

Katie John looked down at the brown hound running around her, licking at her legs, bobbing white spot signaling "Come on!" She caught the spot in her hand for a moment.

"Heavens, no!" she told the policeman. "He's the dearest dog in the world!"

Strange Noises

"He seems perfectly well now." That was Mother's voice.

"It would mean twenty-five dollars more a month." Dad's voice.

Katie John was in the parlor, tracing a map of the United States for social studies. Her parents were still sitting at the dining-room table drinking coffee after supper. They were talking about Cousin Ben and the Money Problem. Cousin Ben was in his room with the door shut—he kept it shut all the time now. He'd gotten through February all right, March was almost gone, and still he showed no signs of ending his visit. Another publisher had turned down Dad's book about the newspaper business, and money was scarce as ever at the Tucker house. It certainly would help if they could rent out Cousin Ben's room.

"Maybe they'll buy your new book," Mother was saying. "Why won't you tell me what it's about, now that it's done?"

"It's just some nonsense, Abby. I don't want you to get your hopes up. No, we'll simply have to tell Ben

Orlick good-by. You cook up a good supper tomorrow night, Abby, and after he's eaten I'll explain that we need to rent his room."

The telephone rang, and Katie went to answer it. Someone wanted to speak to Mr. Peters. Instead of yelling down the basement stairs she stepped to the speaking-tube hole in the parlor wall. Katie was very proud of herself for figuring out this system. The renters received many telephone calls, and at first Katie and her mother wore themselves out running up and down stairs calling them to the phone. Then Katie John had thought of the speaking-tube system Great-Aunt Emily had had built into the walls of the house years ago.

Katie had found it last summer when she'd curiously stuck her finger in the china-rimmed hole in the parlor wall and then couldn't get it out. Mother had to soap her finger loose. Later she and Sue had fun with the speaking-tube system. She would stay by the parlor hole, while Sue went up to one of the third-floor bedrooms. Then Katie would blow into the china mouthpiece of the hole, and that would make a piece of tin whistle in the hole in Sue's room, telling her someone wanted to speak to her. Sue would then open her end of the speaking tube by turning a tiny handle on her mouthpiece. By putting their mouths to the holes, the girls could talk across the house to each other, as if they had their own private telephone system.

Now Katie and her mother used the speaking tubes to call the renters to the phone. Of course they had to puff awfully hard at the parlor hole to make the little whistles blow in all the rooms. And of course every renter had to answer at his or her hole to find out who was wanted. But Mother admitted it was easier than climbing to the third floor to call the men to the telephone, and Katie thought it was lots more fun.

Katie started to blow into the mouthpiece to summon Mr. Peters. What was that sound? A tiny high whine, like a mosquito coming in for attack. She looked around but the sound wasn't in the parlor. It was coming from the china hole. Katie John put her ear to the hole. Yes, now she could bear it better, a shrill buzz. Was it the wind in the speaking tubes? Was someone blowing into his speaking hole? It didn't sound quite the same as the tin whistle.

"Hello?" Katie said.

No one answered. The whine continued. She'd call Mr. Peters and see what happened. She blew hard into the speaking tube.

Presently Gladys answered, "Yes?"

"It's for Mr. Peters," Katie said.

"Hello?" That was Mr. Peabody.

"It's for Mr. Peters," Katie repeated patiently.

In the background the strange sound went on.

"Whatya want?" Buster's voice.

"Tell your father he's wanted on the telephone, please."

No more voices in the speaking tube now, but still she

could hear the whine. Oh, well, it was probably nothing. Katie finished her homework while Mr. Peters was talking on the telephone in the front hall. After she'd put her books away and the riverman had gone back downstairs, though, she decided to listen at the hole once more.

Yes, the whine was still there. Ur-ee. It seemed to get higher, like a vacuum cleaner revving up. Maybe the handle on one of the renters' speaking holes was stuck open. Maybe the sound came from one of the rooms. But none of the renters had a vacuum cleaner. There, the whine stopped. And now there was a whispering sound. Whss-ssk-ssk. She couldn't make out the words, but someone was whispering by a speaking hole.

A prickle ran up Katie's arms, and her feet suddenly felt cold. Why should anyone be whispering? *What was going on in her house?*

Now the shrill sound started again, drowning out the whispering. At last Katie John took her ear away from the hole, her ear still ringing with the whine. She rubbed her cold hands. She'd always thought such an old house should have a mystery, but she didn't like this. This was frightening. All of the renters seemed so ordinary. Yet someone in this house was doing something very strange. Someone was not what he pretended to be.

She had to find that whine. She'd listen at all the doors, and when she found the sound—well—Katie took a big breath—she'd knock on the door.

She tiptoed up the back stairs to the landing by Gladys'

and Pearl's room. The radio was going full blast. "Until I met chew," hollered a hillbilly singer. She could hear the women talking, but not what they said. Everything as usual in this room.

Or was it all a cover up? Maybe the women played the radio all the time to drown out the other sound, the whine. Suppose Pearl and Gladys were spies! Spying on—on the dam in the river above Barton's Bluff. And the whine was some kind of high-frequency radio signal to their comrades somewhere. The whispering was one of the women talking into the secret radio, telling what she'd spied on today. Pearl and Gladys were here in disguise. In their home country they were beautiful, mysterious women. No, that was too much. No matter what Pearl and Gladys were, they weren't beautiful.

Well, she'd soon find out what they were doing. Katie John knocked on the door. Gladys opened it, a dish towel in her hand. Pearl was sitting in a rocking chair, reading a newspaper. She didn't put the paper down, only looked over the top of it.

"Well?" said Gladys.

"Uh, do you need any firewood?"

"For once, no." Gladys shut the door.

They'd looked innocent enough. Still, Pearl might have been hiding the secret radio in her lap behind the newspaper. Well, she'd check the other rooms.

Katie went into the front part of the second floor toward Miss Howell's apartment. Her teacher and Miss

Julia had two big rooms and a bath. No light showed under their doors. Katie listened. No sound from their rooms. They must be out.

Or were they in there in the dark, with the whine quickly turned off when they heard her coming? Katie knocked. But of course they wouldn't answer even if they were there, if they had something to hide.

This was awful. She didn't want to believe her dear teacher could do something strange and bad. How could she even suspect her in the first place!

Katie John tiptoed on up to the third floor. Only Mr. Watkins and Mr. Peabody up here. She listened at Mr. Watkins' door. No whine. Snores. He was sleeping. Or was he pretending?

Every night he went out. Did they know for sure that he was working as a night watchman? Mr. Peters had brought him up from the flour mill. Maybe they were in something together. What did Mr. Watkins do out in the night? Rob places? Then why the whine?

Oh, she didn't want to suspect him, either, not after he'd been so nice about rescuing her from the roof. She still felt guilty about his tiptoeing down the stairs every night. It was hateful of her to believe bad things about him, or anyone in the house.

And yet, she had heard the whine. Something secret was going on right here in her own safe house.

She moved on to Mr. Peabody's door. His light was out, and there was no sound from within. Now that was strange. He'd answered the speaking-tube whistle a little bit ago, and she hadn't heard him go out. Surely he hadn't gone to bed so early.

And now that she thought of it, there was something else strange about Mr. Peabody. He'd started paying his rent again. All of a sudden he had money. Maybe he was counterfeiting it! She didn't know what kind of sound counterfeiting machinery would make. Maybe it whined.

Katie John stood in the dark hall. She ought to knock on his door now. But the prickles were raising goose bumps on her arms again. What would happen when he opened the door? What would he do? What would she see?

This was something for a grownup. She'd tell Dad. But as soon as she formed words in her mind, she knew how silly it would sound to Dad. He'd say she had no reason for connecting the whine with Mr. Peabody, and he wouldn't want to knock on the man's door because he'd probably gone to bed.

Yet she was sure the mystery man was Mr. Peabody. She'd have to find out more about him. Tomorrow was Saturday. When she cleaned his room she'd look for counterfeiting machinery or whatever made the whine. Of course, she hadn't noticed anything odd in his room last Saturday, but then she wasn't looking. Maybe it was inside the window-seat cupboard. Or maybe he'd just brought it in this week.

And when Mr. Peabody went out tomorrow morning, she'd follow him.

When Katie got back downstairs she listened again at the parlor speaking-tube hole. No whine. No sound at all. She'd expected that. No point in listening at any more doors. Mr. Peabody or whoever it was had stopped for the night. She ran to the telephone and called up Sue.

"Sue, we've got a real mystery!" she whispered into the telephone. "Come up first thing in the morning and help me."

Of course Sue wanted to know all about it, but Katie whispered that she was afraid someone would hear. She'd tell Sue in the morning.

That night Katie John locked her bedroom door for the first time. Long into the night she lay awake listening for unusual sounds.

As a result she overslept the next morning. She was just getting dressed when Sue arrived, eyes big with questions. She told Sue about the whine and the whispers and about listening at the doors. When she came to the part about Mr. Peabody's dark room, Sue said in a very small voice, "Katie John, I don't think I want to explore this mystery."

"You've got to help," Katie insisted. "Besides, it's broad daylight now. Nothing can hurt us."

Sue started to protest more, but Katie grabbed her arm. "Ssh! Listen!"

Sue jumped and squeaked.

"Oh, silly," Katie John laughed. "I just meant, listen, someone's coming downstairs. I think it's Mr. Peabody."

The girls peeked out Katie's door, looking along the hall to the front of the house. Yes, short, skinny Mr. Peabody was going out the front door.

"Come on!" Katie pulled Sue along. "We've got to follow him!"

The girls waited at the front gate until Mr. Peabody was well down the block. Katie John pretended she was swinging on the iron gate in case he looked back.

"I think you ought to tell your folks," Sue said.

"No time. He's almost to the corner. Come on."

Katie John hurried down the sidewalk, dragging Sue with her. Mr. Peabody turned the corner, so Katie ran. When the girls reached the corner, they could see that he was going toward Main Street. Keeping a careful half of a block behind, they followed him. Was he looking back?

"Pretend you're looking in the store window!" Katie muttered, wheeling to stare in a plumbing shop. "Now it's all right. He's not looking at us."

They went on. There weren't many people on Main Street this early in the morning, and it was easy to keep the small man in sight.

"Look! He's going into the supermarket," Sue said.

"Now why? Maybe he's trying to lose us. Hurry!"

The girls dashed ahead to the grocery store, which seemed to have just opened. The aisles were almost empty of people. Yet Mr. Peabody had disappeared. Katie and Sue hunted up and down between the rows of bread and pickles and canned peas. They even peeked through the swinging doors back into the butcher shop.

"He's given us the slip," Katie said.

"No, look. Oh, Katie!" Sue was laughing.

There at the checkout counter was Mr. Peabody, wearing a long apron. He was working here.

"Oh!" Katie John could hardly believe the little man was doing such an ordinary thing. She'd been so sure he was headed on a secret mission. Maybe this explained why he could pay his rent now. He had a new job. She didn't know whether she was disappointed or relieved.

"I guess he isn't the mystery man," she said. "But— but then we still don't know who made the whining sound."

She didn't feel a bit better. Now she might have to suspect someone in her house that she liked. Suspicion. It was a nasty sensation, made her feel dirty somehow. Yet she couldn't just forget about the strange noises in the speaking tubes. She had to solve the mystery, for how could she rest easy, knowing that one person in the house was not what he seemed?

"Come on, Sue, let's go before Mr. Peabody sees us and wonders what we're doing."

Today was Saturday, Katie's day to clean the renters' rooms. Sue said she'd help, and the girls decided to search for clues in the rooms as they worked.

As it turned out, however, the girls weren't able to get into all the rooms. Gladys was home and opened her door only wide enough to take the clean sheets and towels Katie had brought. Mr. Peters was at work, but Buster was in and out of the apartment all morning getting dog biscuits to teach Heavenly Spot to speak for his food. Katie wasn't supposed to clean in there, anyway, for the riverman kept his rooms as spotless as a freshly-swabbed deck. And although Miss Howell was out, Miss Julia was in their apartment. Katie John was glad she couldn't search there. She didn't know how she could face her teacher at school after snooping through her things.

In Mr. Watkins' room the girls couldn't find a thing to get excited about. It seemed to be an ordinary working-man's home—work clothes hanging in the closet, a few photographs of people on the dresser, canned food and bread on a shelf under his hot plate. Katie John couldn't bring herself to look in his dresser drawers. It didn't seem right.

Mr. Peabody's room, though cluttered, seemed innocent enough, too. Sue did find a knife in a sheath thrown down on the window seat among the magazines. For a moment the girls wondered what such a mousy-looking little man would want with such a big knife. But on examining it they decided it was just a hunting knife.

Katie John threw the used sheets down the stair well, after checking to see there was no one below. She turned to Sue, sighing in exasperation.

"That's all of the renters' rooms, and we haven't found a thing."

"Have you listened for the noises today?"

"No. Let's listen."

First Katie and then Sue put an ear to the speaking-tube hole in Mr. Peabody's room, but the speaking tube was silent. They went downstairs to listen at the hole in the parlor. Not a sound.

"Well, let's get Cousin Ben's bedroom cleaned," Katie said, "and then we can think what to do next."

Cousin Ben was out for his morning's walk. Sue straightened up the room, while Katie John vacuumed. Usually Mother cleaned this room, but Katie had talked her into doing all the washing today so the girls would be free to search the rooms. It wasn't that she hadn't wanted Mother to know what she was doing. It was just that a person doesn't want a grownup looking over her shoulder when she's hunting down a mystery. She might have to tell Mother and Dad, though, because she couldn't think of any more ways to solve this mystery.

She ran the vacuum cleaner into the long closet. It was so big it had a window at the end. Now what was that hanging from a hook on the wall? Something roundish, with cords hanging down from it. Why, it was some kind of small motor, and—

"Sue!"

Katie John switched off the vacuum cleaner as Sue came running.

"I think I've found it! Look!"

The girls examined the contraption. It was a motor,

all right, and at the end of one of its cords was a thing that looked like a dentist's drill. Another cord had a foot pedal hanging at its end, and the third cord was for plugging the whole thing into an electric socket.

"I've never seen this thing before," Katie whispered. "Let's plug it in and see what happens."

There were no electric outlets in the closet, so the girls carried the contraption out to the bedroom. Katie John plugged the cord to the only wall socket. Nothing happened. Oh. She stepped on the foot pedal. And the motor started with a thin, shrill whine. It sounded just like a vacuum cleaner starting up. The harder she pressed on the pedal, the higher the whine. Katie took her foot off the pedal and stared at Sue.

"This is it! This is what made the sound! And see, here's a speaking-tube hole in the wall right above the electric socket."

Just as she'd figured, the little handle on the hole was stuck open. That's why she'd been able to hear the motor.

Cousin Ben! So Cousin Ben Orlick was the mystery man. She hadn't even thought of suspecting him. Yet, why not? What did they really know about him? Only what he'd told them. Mother hadn't even remembered him when he'd arrived. Maybe this explained why he'd stayed here all winter. He was hiding out. He was using their house to do something secret with this motor and this drill.

"But what has he been making with it?" she said aloud. "What's it for?"

"For sharpening the noses of snoopy little girls."

Sue gave a little shriek and Katie John whirled to see Cousin Ben standing in the doorway. His eyes were snapping and his chin whiskers bristled, he was so mad.

"I—I'm going to tell my mother." Katie made a dash for the door.

The old man blocked her off. "Oh, no, you're not. You young'uns stay right here. I'll tell Abigail my own way." Quickly he stepped out of the door and locked it from the outside.

They were prisoners. He was going to make his getaway. No, Katie could hear his footsteps going down the hall to the basement stairs.

"Let's climb out a window," Sue said, about to cry.

"Wait. I think he really is going after Mother."

Voices were coming up the basement stairs and along the hall, Mother making bewildered murmurs as Cousin Ben's voice crackled on, "—been working till who laid the rail, making something. I was going to give it to you at suppertime, but these young'uns had to go poking around."

The key turned in the lock, and Mother and Cousin Ben walked into the bedroom.

"Katie John Tucker!" Mother said.

Well, for goodness' sakes, what had she done wrong now? It was Cousin Ben that—

He took a small package out of his dresser drawer and handed it to Mother.

"There. Meant to make a speech at the supper table. No matter. Just something to say thanks for taking care of an old man when he was sick." He stuck his hands in his pockets and looked out the window.

So that's all it was. He'd been making a present for Mother. Probably some dumb thing like a wooden box.

But Mother was gasping, "Oh, Ben!" She had the package open, and Katie John and Sue ran to look. Lying on cotton in the small box was a pair of glowing green earrings.

"They—look like—emeralds," Mother said in a hushed voice.

"Are. Had 'em left over from my stock."

Mother lifted one of the lovely square emeralds and fitted it to her ear.

"Mother, it's beautiful!"

She meant more than that. It was Mother who was beautiful, with the green glow against her cheek. Her hair shone blacker, and Katie'd never noticed it before, but Mother's eyes had a green sparkle. Before she'd just looked like a mother, but now—!

Where had Cousin Ben gotten such lovely stones? She turned to stare at the old man. Mother and Sue were staring at him, too. Embarrassed, he jingled the coins in his pockets.

"Had a little jewelry store down home once," he said.

"I don't tell folks because they always want me to give them something."

He'd gone out of business long ago, he explained, but he'd kept a few nice things from his stock. He'd borrowed the small motor from a jewelry store downtown to cut the holes in the metal for mounting the emeralds.

Mother was protesting, "But I was happy to— These are too much—I can't take them—"

Cousin Ben stuck out his chin whiskers. "You keep 'em. Guess I can give something away if I want to."

Mother laughed then. "Cousin Ben Orlick, you're a dear!" She gave him a smacking kiss on his cheek.

He grinned with delight even though he tried to sound crusty as he said, "All right, all right. Clear out now. I've got to get this motor back to the store."

The girls went to Katie's room to talk about it all.

"My, I was scared," Sue chattered in relief now that it was over. "For a minute there I thought he—"

"What beautiful earrings!" Katie sighed happily.

And what a relief to stop looking at each renter, wondering which one was pretending. They were just ordinary people, with an ordinary mix-mux of good and ornery. There'd been a secret in the house, all right, but it was a kind secret.

"But what was the whispering sound?" she said suddenly. "Oh, I know," she answered herself, laughing. "I'll bet Cousin Ben was talking to himself while he worked."

That figured. He talked so much, he probably even talked to himself when he was alone.

She could hear Mother and Dad in the kitchen next to her room. Mother was showing the emeralds to Dad and laughing helplessly.

"We just can't ask Ben Orlick to leave now," she said. "Imagine! Emeralds! When we need money so. Well, we may go to the poorhouse, but your wife will go in style, with emeralds in her ears!"

Katie John's Knight

It was spring, no doubt about it. The gray landscape of winter was gone, and there was color everywhere. Daffodils nodded yellow-bright against green grass, golden forsythia bushes feathered out in every yard. The country children at school reported that the woods were thick with violets. On the river the ice had broken up, and towboats were beginning to pass Barton's Bluff again. Mr. Peters and Buster would be leaving soon, the riverman back to his boat, Buster back to his aunt in Iowa.

One April evening as soft as May Katie John and Sue walked to church for choir practice. The grass still sparkled from an afternoon shower, and the robins were busy on the lawns in the last light after sunset.

"We almost don't need coats," Sue said, shrugging at hers.

Katie John frowned down at the knee-length stockings her mother had made her wear all winter. "Tomorrow I'm going to wear anklets to school," she declared.

She was glad to be going somewhere tonight. There was a fresh, waiting feeling to the air, as if something were about to happen. And she felt different, somehow.

Perhaps a little like Cathy—no, that was silly. Not like Cathy. But not quite like herself, either.

The girls entered the church's parish hall. It was the custom for the children's choir to practice with a piano in the parish hall, rather than in the church. Some of the children from school went to Katie's church and sang in the choir. Howard Bunch and Sammy and Edwin Jones were setting up chairs, the first two boys horsing around at it, Edwin going about it quietly. Betsy Ann was putting out hymnals on the chairs. Priscilla Simmons didn't come to this church. Her family had gone to another church for generations.

"Here, Katie," Howard Bunch called, holding a chair for her to sit down.

"Oh—thanks." Katie gave him a startled smile. How nice to be treated like a lady.

She sat down—and down. Bump! Her bottom hit the floor with a jar. Howard had pulled the chair out from under her. Oh, her hip hurt so! She was going to cry. Automatic tears filled her eyes, and she couldn't keep her mouth from twisting up.

"Haw, haw, haw!" Howard was roaring. "Contact!"

The stinker! Katie John got control of herself and stood up, Sue helping her and murmuring, "Are you hurt?"

With as much dignity as possible while holding her sore hip, Katie John said, "You're no gentleman, Howard Bunch!"

"Who wants to be?" Howard went right on laughing and looking pleased with his joke.

Why, he didn't even care that she'd actually been hurt. Sammy was laughing, too. Katie John limped to another chair and sat her throbbing hip down carefully. She looked at Edwin Jones. At least he wasn't laughing. He smiled at her as if he were sorry.

Well, then, if he was sorry, and he liked her, why didn't he do something to Howard? Of course, that was too much to expect. Edwin was slow and quiet, and besides, Howard was bigger than he was.

The lady who directed the choir came in and the choir practice proceeded. Katie could hardly sing. Not only did her hip hurt, but she hurt inside, too. It's not very nice to have someone turn around and do something mean to you when you're expecting a kindness.

When the singing was done, Katie John hobbled out, Sue's arm around her.

"Aw, quit acting, Katie," Howard called behind her. "You aren't hurt that bad."

As the boys came out the door behind the girls, Katie heard Edwin mutter something to Howard.

"Why should I?" Howard said loudly. "It was only a joke."

"I said, you apologize to Katie John," Edwin repeated in a clear voice.

Howard squared around to him on the church lawn. "Who's gonna make me?"

Edwin's face was white. "I will."

"Yeahh?" Howard grabbed Edwin's shoulders for the half-hearted wrestling around that the boys called fighting.

Edwin didn't fight that way. His skinny arms snaked out in a wild punch right in Howard's face. Katie John gasped as Howard rocked back. Oh, goodness, Howard's nose was bleeding.

"Why, you—you punk!" Howard rushed at Edwin, pounding with his fists.

The girls screamed and Sammy and the other boys happily yelled "Fight! Fight!"

Howard's rush had knocked Edwin to the ground. He twisted, trying to get out from under Howard's pounding.

"Say uncle!" the big boy grunted.

Edwin punched at Howard's face again, but he was in an awkward position, being flat on his back. Howard's fists came down on his head.

"Stop it! Stop it!" Katie shrieked. He'd kill Edwin!

"Say uncle!" Howard demanded.

The choir lady ran out the door. "Boys, boys!" she cried. "Stop it! Stop this very minute!"

She hauled Howard off of Edwin, and the boys obeyed grown-up authority, even though they still faced each other breathing angry gasps.

"He—" Howard began.

"I don't want to hear a word of what it's about," she declared. "You go straight home, Howard Bunch, or I'll tell your mother. You, too, Edwin Jones. Fighting on the church lawn, for mercy sakes!"

Edwin walked off, still breathing hard. Katie started to go after him, but Sammy and another boy began a chant.

"Katie's got a boy friend! Katie's got a boy friend!"

Oh, those boys! Katie John wheeled and walked away with Sue.

"Boys are just awful!" Sue exclaimed with unusual heat. "Sometimes I wish they'd just disappear off the earth."

"Yes!"

All, except maybe Edwin. Katie John let out a big breath. Now that it was over, a little smile began at the tips of her mouth. Who'd ever have thought she'd have a boy fighting for her tonight? Just like a knight going to battle for his lady. How good Edwin was, not a scaredy-cat, after all. Maybe he took his time about what he was going to do, but when he did, wham! And she hadn't even thanked him. After a knight battled for his lady, she always gave him a reward. Her handkerchief, or something. Well, tomorrow—

The next morning Katie John packed two extra cupcakes in her lunch. First thing when she got to school she'd thank Edwin for being so thoughtful and brave. He really was a hero, when you thought how much bigger Howard was than Edwin. No matter that he hadn't won the fight. It was the brave, knight-like spirit that counted. At lunch she'd give him the cupcakes.

On the way to school Katie John felt trembly-excited. "Thank you for defending me, Edwin," she'd say graciously. Edwin would be a stalwart figure smiling kindly down at her, his hair shining in the sun. Vaguely she pictured a soft veil floating from her head, and Edwin in silver armor . . .

She hunted on the school playground until she saw Edwin. He was alone, idly bouncing a basketball on the ground near a hoop. But—he looked so little, not at all the way she'd been thinking of him. Just a skinny boy with fuzzy yellow chicken hair. His jeans weren't very clean, and neither were his hands. Why, he looked downright grubby.

Edwin Jones was no knight.

Katie John felt blank, as if a color movie had suddenly gone black and white. Oh, well, she ought to thank the boy, anyway. She started toward him.

"Katie's got a boy friend, Katie's got a boy friend!"

Sammy and Howard and some other boys were singing the chant and laughing.

Edwin turned red. He saw Katie, frowned, and walked away quickly.

Well! If he was ashamed of her . . . He was just a scaredy-cat, after all. And a grubby, messy boy, besides.

All through school Katie John carefully kept her eyes

away from Edwin. The sight of him was too nauseating. And at lunchtime she ate the extra cupcakes, forcing down every last crumb.

The next day was Saturday, and the good weather held. Katie John and Sue had planned to ride their bikes out to Crystal Glen that afternoon to pick violets. Sue had heard that white violets were growing along the creek in the Glen, and the purple violets there were extra big.

After lunch Saturday Katie John called Heavenly Spot, got onto her bike—The Explorer, she'd named it—and coasted down the sidewalk to Sue's house. When Sue came to the door, however, she shook her head.

"I can't go," she said. "My California aunt just drove in, and I have to stay home and hear all about the orange groves and how wonderful Los Angeles is."

"Poor you. Well, I think I'll go out to Crystal Glen anyway. Do you mind? I haven't got anything else to do."

"No, you go ahead," Sue said generously.

"I'll bring you some violets," Katie promised, wheeling off down the street.

Heavenly Spot trotted along beside her, eager for the outing. Katie smiled at the white tip of his tail bobbing along.

"You're all the company I need, Spot," she told him. Spot ran close to lick her leg as she pumped the pedals.

Crystal Glen was a woodsy hollow on the other side of town. It took its name from the glittering geode rocks found there. A dirt road led around to it, but Katie knew of a short cut through the cemetery. Not the little pioneer cemetery she'd found on the river bluff, but the big graveyard for Barton's Bluff.

Katie John rode into the cemetery between open iron gates. To the left was a whole hillside of white markers, row upon row of them. That part was a national cemetery, where soldiers were buried. Slowly she coasted down the winding road through the graveyard. She thought it was even prettier here than in the park. Flowering bushes bloomed on many family plots. It was like a well-kept woods in these hills and hollows, so many big old trees, thick with birds. And the birds sang freely, undisturbed here, the only sound in this peaceful place.

At the bottom of the lane she came to a stone bench by a square marble gravestone. The way to Crystal Glen lay up over the next hill and beyond the edge of the cemetery. She decided to rest a bit before going on, and sat down on the stone bench. Heavenly Spot went nosing off after a flurry of squirrel. "In memory of Mildred Sears, 1896," read a metal plaque on the arm of the bench. Katie John leaned back to listen to the cool green stillness of the cemetery. "Hooo, hooo," a mourning dove called off in the trees somewhere, not sadly, but gently, just the right sound in this spot.

Across the road stood a life-sized angel. Katie regarded the statue. The Black Angel, the kids called it, for the metal—bronze or something—had turned dark. There was a tale that the metal had turned black for some sad, mysterious reason. However, the Black Angel was better known for a local custom: when teenagers kissed under the Black Angel, that meant they were going steady. Kissing—ugh. Katie's stomach squirmed at the very idea.

"Here, boy! Come back here! Wreeet!"

Katie saw her dog tearing across a hillside of graves, with a boy whistling and running after him. The boy was Edwin Jones. What on earth! What was Edwin Jones doing in the cemetery, and why was he chasing her dog?

And here she was, sitting practically right under the Black Angel. As if she was sitting here waiting for someone to— Oh, goodness, she'd just die if that nasty Edwin found her here. He hadn't seen her yet, he was running with his back to her. Where could she hide?

Farther along the lane stood several small stone buildings. Katie John ran to the nearest one. Iron grille gates to the building stood open. She rushed in, yanking the gates shut after her. Now if Heavenly Spot just wouldn't lead Edwin here . . .

It was damp and dusky inside. When Katie's eyes adjusted to the dark, she saw metal name plates along the walls. This must be some kind of family tomb. Maybe she shouldn't be in here. All sounds of Edwin and the dog were gone. Katie pushed at the iron gates. Stubborn things. They were sticking. She pushed harder, but they wouldn't open. Something was holding them. She looked down and saw that the two gates were jammed together inside a metal catch in the stone floor. When she'd slammed them shut so hard, she'd pulled them right over the gate stop, and now they were wedged tight.

Oh, how idiotic. Why did this kind of thing always happen to her? If she could lift one of the gates over the metal catch . . . Katie pulled, but the iron grille wouldn't move.

How was she going to get out? Would she just have to stay here until someone came along next Memorial Day?

The sound of feet came pounding along the dirt lane. Thank goodness, Spot was hunting her out. Edwin must have caught him just then, because the feet stopped and she heard Edwin talking to the dog.

"Where you going, fella? Don't you know you can't run in the cemetery, hey? You're a pretty good dog, though."

Katie John peered through the grillwork and saw the boy just down the lane, tousling her dog. Spot had rolled onto his back with joy at the attention. Dumb dog. Couldn't he tell Edwin was nothing but a nasty boy?

Nasty or not, however, she'd better call Edwin if she was ever going to get out of this tomb.

"Edwin," she called in a small voice. "Edwin Jones."

The boy jerked up and looked around, his eyes startled. Katie choked down a sudden snicker. He must be scared to hear his name called by a voice from a tomb.

But Edwin had seen her. He was coming over.

"Katie John! What are you doing in there?"

"Oh," she said airily, "just looking around." She added, "Uh—the gates are stuck. Could you maybe get them open?"

Edwin stared at her. At least he didn't laugh. His long face stayed as solemn as ever.

"Sure." Not a word about how did she get them jammed. He bent and tried to lift the gates, without effect. "Need something to pry with," he muttered.

Katie John watched him curiously as he hunted along the lane for a strong stick.

"What are *you* doing here?" she asked finally.

"Live here," Edwin called back.

Now it was Katie's turn to stare, as Edwin came back with a stick.

"My dad's the caretaker," he explained. "We live in that house over there." He pointed to a small brick house set in the trees beyond the soldiers' graves. "I thought you knew."

Oh, dear, he thought—he thought she'd come out here looking for him! Chasing after him. Her face burned.

"No, I didn't know." Her voice came out too loud. Firmly she added, "I was on my way to Crystal Glen."

"Oh."

Edwin's face was flushed, too, probably from heaving against one of the gates with the stick. The iron grilles moved a little, so that now they weren't jammed across each other, but they still were caught behind the catch.

For something to say, Katie asked, "Don't you mind living in the cemetery?"

"No. I like it here." He glanced at her and then looked down at his work.

"Must be like having your own private park."

"Yes, but it's more than that. It's— Aw, nothing." He scowled at the stick, prying away.

Katie John remembered how she'd laughed when he said he wanted to be a pirate. Maybe he was afraid she'd laugh now.

"It's what?" she prompted him.

"Oh—just that I like to read the gravestones. You can learn a lot about the history of the town, just from reading the inscriptions."

Edwin's face turned a brighter red. Well, there was nothing funny about what he'd said. She liked to read the inscriptions, too, and she told him so.

The red faded from Edwin's face. He stopped working to explain himself carefully. "Maybe you think it's just grave-snooping, but men do it, too. I've read books about it. Archaeology, it's called, digging up Indian burial grounds or ruins in Greece, to learn about ancient civilizations. I'd like to go hunting old temples in the jungles of Central America. Or maybe be the one to find another pyramid in the Sahara Desert."

"How could anyone miss a pyramid? They stick up so high."

"I guess you don't know much about it." Edwin smiled as he started heaving away with the stick again. "The way the sand drifts over there, it could hide a whole pyramid. There's lots we don't know about what happened centuries ago."

He looked up again, his eyes bright. "You know, Katie John, that's the best kind of exploring there is left in the world. Think of all the mysteries to solve!"

Katie's imagination caught fire. "Oh, Edwin, I wish I could go exploring with you!"

She could have bitten her tongue. Now he'd think she was crazy about him, wanting to tag after him.

But Edwin seemed to be thinking it over slowly, as he always did. "I guess you could," he said. "I've read of women archaeologists, too."

He gave a mighty heave, and one iron gate lifted over the metal catch at last. He pulled the gate open, and Katie stepped out.

Edwin had saved her. Yesterday he'd fought for her, and today he'd released her, like a knight saving a lady from a dungeon in a castle.

She looked at the fuzzy-haired boy with the long face and blinked her eyes. No, that was a lot of silliness. Edwin Jones was no knight. He was just a boy. But he wasn't too awful a boy, at that. Down underneath he had something—imagination, maybe—that she'd been missing in Sue. Not that she'd trade Sue for any old boy. Still . . .

"I know it isn't as good as hunting ancient temples,"

she offered, "but I know of a little pioneer cemetery I could show you someday."

Edwin had been watching her, too. Now his long face brightened. "Okay, Katie," he said, actually smiling.

Katie ran toward her bike, whistling for Spot.

"Oh—thanks for everything," she called back.

"See you at school," Edwin answered.

Katie John smiled to herself. She had a feeling Edwin Jones wouldn't frown and walk away from her at school any more, no matter what those dumb boys chanted.

One Big Happy Family

After school Katie John parted with Sue at Sue's house and walked on up the block looking at her own house more closely than she had for some time. Tall trees waved leafy green around the red-brick walls, and old-fashioned white snowball bushes dripped blossoms by the porch. It was a good old house, friendly and solid. Yet it would start emptying soon. Miss Howell and her sister would be moving back to their farmhouse by the river next weekend, and Mr. Peters and Buster were leaving the following Monday, when Mr. Peters' towboat was due up the river. That left only Gladys and Pearl, Mr. Watkins and Mr. Peabody, and Cousin Ben. That Cousin Ben! He must simply be planning to stay with them forever. Miss Crackenberry was surprised. She'd told Mother that Ben Orlick had never visited Great-Aunt Emily this long into spring. Katie was beginning to wonder if he even had a sister Louisey to go back to. Certainly the Tuckers could never ask him to leave now that he'd given Mother those beautiful earrings.

It was still a lovely Monday afternoon, however, until

Katie John went into her house and discovered that Buster was lost.

Mother had cobwebs in her hair from looking in the corner behind the piano just as Katie came in.

"I've looked everywhere for that child!" she exclaimed. "I don't see how he could be so gone."

"Maybe he's at the 'Y,' swimming."

"I called there," Mother said. "I should have known he was up to something. When I was out weeding the iris he went past me with his eyes down, the way he does when he doesn't want you to know what he's planning."

Katie John said she'd hunt for him. First she checked at the homes of his playmates in the neighborhood, but none of the children had seen Buster since school let out.

"Now where did that little skunk go?" she muttered. She crossed a street along the bluff and saw the river sparkling below. "Uh-*huh!* I bet he's gone to the river."

She hurried to the edge of the bluff and looked down. No sign of Buster, but a trail led down the hill, and she followed it. Of course he could be anywhere along the riverbank—if he was even here. Katie followed the shore around a bend, and there up ahead, on a little spit of land sticking out into the river, was Buster. He had his shoes off.

"Buster Peters! What do you think you're doing?"

Buster jerked around at the sound of her voice, then stuck his chin out.

"Wadin'. 'Bout to."

He stepped toward the water's edge.

"Are you bats? The river's too cold to wade in yet."

"No, t'ain't. I go ever' year 'bout this time. Sign that winter's over."

He stuck his toe into the water, winced, and waded in ankle-deep. Katie John didn't stop him. She understood. He was celebrating spring. It was sort of a nice idea, at that. She looked at the scene before her, the water lapping easily against the little piece of land, almost an island, it was, with one small tree leafed out, and one bird singing a soft, late-afternoon song in the tree. And one small boy sloshing in the edges of the wide river.

Katie John took off her shoes.

"Oh, it's cold!" she cried as the sharp water curled around her toes.

"Feels good, huh?" Buster squished his feet in the sand below the water.

Katie John shivered in delight. "Feels as if my feet were getting a fresh cool drink of water."

"Yeah. Kinda wakes 'em up for summer."

The last long rays from the setting sun warmed the river as the children waded around the bit of land, up to their shins in Mississippi. At last the sun disappeared behind the bluff, and Katie's feet ached with the cold.

As she and Buster wiped their feet on the grass, Katie said, "You know, Buster, this is a pretty nice thing to do every spring."

"Yeah." Buster's eyes sparkled at her briefly. "Fergot

to tell ya. I catch cold from wadin' every spring, too."

Katie only laughed, but Buster was right. That night she heard him in the basement apartment below, complaining about a sore throat. Once in the night she woke a little and heard Mr. Peters stirring around below, and early in the morning she heard him come upstairs to use the telephone. He was calling a doctor.

Later, as Katie got up, she heard a strange man talking downstairs. That must be the doctor. She was about to go see what was happening when Mother came to her door and explained. Buster had diphtheria. It was a very mild case, and Buster would be all right, but the doctor wanted to talk to the renters. Katie was to go around and ask all of them to come down to the parlor.

Katie John worried as she pulled on her clothes. It was all her fault, letting him wade in that cold water. Who'd have thought a little bit of water . . . Why, she didn't even have a sore throat.

She hurried along the halls, knocking on doors, explaining that Buster had diphtheria, and she didn't know why, but the doctor wanted to see everybody in the parlor. Miss Howell and Miss Julia were already dressed and eating breakfast, Mr. Peabody was getting ready for work, and Mr. Watkins had just come home from work. Cousin Ben grumbled, though, at being waked up so early, and Gladys and Pearl must have just rolled out of bed, too, because they looked even more stringy and bleary first thing in the morning.

When everyone was assembled in the parlor and talk-ing in hushed voices about "that poor little Buster," the doctor came upstairs with Mr. Peters.

"Now, the little fellow is going to be all right," the doctor said. "He'll be on the mend in a couple of days. But I'm afraid you'll all have to be confined to the house for five days."

Even mild diphtheria was catching, he said, so the house would be under quarantine.

"Everyone must have two negative throat cultures before release, and I'll—"

"Quarantine!" Gladys exclaimed. "What you mean, can't go out? I gotta be at work in half an hour."

"Yeah. If I don't work, I don't get paid," Mr. Pea-body put in.

Everyone was talking at once, Mr. Peters looked embar-rassed, and Dad kept saying, "Now, folks, now, folks, we must listen to the doctor."

The doctor walked to the door. "I'm sorry, everybody, but that's the law. Nobody goes in or out of this house for five days."

Katie John ran after him. "I let him wade in the river. Was that what caused—"

"No," the doctor reassured her. "I think he was already coming down with it."

"Little fella never had diphtheria shots," said Mr. Peters, who had followed them, "we move around so much. Don't you fret none, Katie John. You couldn't have stopped that boy from wadin', anyway. He does it ever' spring."

Relieved, Katie cried, "Wow! No school for the rest of the week."

Then she saw Miss Howell smiling at her. Oh, for goodness' sakes. Her teacher was going to be in quarantine with her, right handy. Just for once she wished Miss Howell didn't live in the same house.

The renters waited around the telephone in the hall to take turns calling their employers.

"Mrs. Tucker, I've got a good mind to make you explain to my boss why I can't come to work," Pearl was saying.

Gladys added to Dad, "You certainly can't expect us to pay the rent this week if we can't work. The idea! Why, I haven't even been near that little—"

She stopped as Mr. Peters went past silently. Katie knew she was about to say "brat," though. The word fairly trembled in the air. Oh, what a grubbly mess this house was going to be all week, everyone cooped up and mad at each other.

Katie John was right. Of course not much happened the first day because everyone was still worried about Buster. Miss Howell set Katie to doing schoolwork, and Mother had the grocery boy leave the orders outside the door. Miss Crackenberry came over at midmorning to find out why the doctor had been there, but when she saw the quarantine sign on the door, she hurried home to telephone Mother instead. By Wednesday morning, how-ever, Buster was sitting up in bed ready to be amused, and everyone else was ready to bite.

Mr. Peabody was mad because he'd run out of detec-tive magazines to read. Gladys and Pearl had a loud quarrel. Cousin Ben wandered around trying to remem-ber if he'd ever had diphtheria shots and talking to Dad while he was trying to write. Finally Dad slammed his typewriter case shut and declared it was impossible to work. And even Miss Howell complained to Mother that she was extremely weary of hearing Gladys' and Pearl's radio all day long.

The house had never seemed so full of people. Before, everyone had gone about his business during the day, and the old house had filled up only in the evenings. Now people clattered in their rooms and wandered rest-lessly up and down the halls. There was always some-one in the front hall using the telephone. And the house was full of bad temper. When polite Mr. Watkins snapped at her on the fourth day, Katie John burst into tears and ran to her room.

Hateful people. Why did we ever rent out rooms in the first place? Can't even call our house our own. Just a houseful of mean, bad-tempered strangers. Great-Grandpa Clark and Great-Aunt Emily would just die if they knew—just die? Katie snorted suddenly through her sobs. How silly. They *are* dead, and in heaven.

She rolled over and stared at the ceiling as a last tear

rolled out of each eye and slid back along her cheek into her hair. The Clarks were dead, and this wasn't a family home any more, that's all there was to it. She supposed she ought to be glad for the renters' money, so she could go on living here.

"If the renters just didn't act so awful," she whispered.

It wasn't fair. She'd put up with them. They ought to act nice. Katie stared at the ceiling some more. At last she sighed. All right, she knew that wasn't quite it. The renters paid their money; they probably thought they had as much right here as she did. They just lived in their rooms, and it wasn't up to them to get along with everyone else. They didn't care whether they were all one happy family.

"But I do," she said to the ceiling.

If they all were going to live here, then she wanted everyone under this roof to be friendly. Otherwise she might as well be living in a public hotel. Just a bare, cold, public rooming house. Not a home at all.

Katie John jumped off her bed and rubbed the dampness from her cheeks as she ran to the kitchen to find Mother.

"Mother, let's give a party tonight! A party for all the renters. Something to pull us together. And maybe Buster could come up for a little while, too."

When Mother had sorted out Katie John's breathless rush of ideas, she said slowly, "I think maybe you've got something there, honey. A party might help us over this trying time, anyway. But Katie—don't expect too much. Remember, it's your idea, making all the household one big family, not the renters' idea."

"I know. But they'll like the party, Mother. I know they will."

Katie busily planned with Mother. They'd have the party around suppertime, and they'd roast hot dogs in the parlor fireplace—Katie thought of that. Mother would make popcorn and bring up the last of the winter's apple cider from the cellar.

"And we can tell stories around the fire and maybe even play charades," Katie said.

Mother smiled and shook her head, repeating, "Don't expect too much. I imagine the grownups would rather just talk."

It was already midafternoon, time to get things organized. While Mother went to the telephone to order a big supply of hot dogs from the grocery store, Katie John began knocking on doors to invite everyone to the party. Buster was eager for the party, especially the popcorn, and his father seemed glad, too. From the look of his tired face, he'd been having quite a time keeping Buster occupied now that he felt better. Mr. Peters said that Buster really shouldn't be out of bed yet, but he'd bring him up for just fifteen minutes.

Then Katie went to Cousin Ben's room. He was not enthusiastic.

"I've seen enough of this pack of folks 'thout sitting around with them all night," he grumbled.

But Katie slyly suggested that he be the chief story-teller at the party, and the old man took a brighter view of the proceedings and agreed to come.

"Will that Miss Julia be there?" he asked. "She likes my stories."

"I'm sure she will," Katie John promised.

She asked her teacher and Miss Julia next, and, as she expected, they thought the plan was a lovely idea. Miss Julia said she'd bring her homemade pickle relish for the hot dogs. Mr. Watkins and Mr. Peabody said they'd come, too.

She'd left Gladys and Pearl to the last. She wished she didn't have to ask them, still wished they didn't even live here. But if you're going to be one big happy family, you've got to include everyone, like them or not.

Katie knocked. Gladys opened the door, and a blare of western music gushed out past her.

"Now what?" she said.

Katie John put on a polite face and explained about the party. Gladys laughed.

"You want to roast hot dogs with the kids?" she called to Pearl, who was reading a magazine.

Pearl shook her head without looking up.

"Nope. Count us out." Gladys started to shut the door.

"Wait. You don't understand. It's a—a happy gather-ing. Everybody has to be there."

"Not us." The door closed.

"Please," Katie begged, then shoved her fingers through her bangs and turned away. She never thought she'd see the day when she'd beg for Gladys' and Pearl's company. All right, let them stay up here by themselves, while everyone else had a wonderful time. Who wanted them!

Just the same, things wouldn't be complete without them. The whole idea was spoiled. Katie John fretted about it as she helped Mother get ready. She'd had a vision of friendly people united under one roof. It just couldn't be if Gladys and Pearl kept apart.

Even though it was warm outside, Dad started a cheerful blaze in the fireplace, and Mother closed the wooden inside shutters to make things seem more cozy and drawn together in the parlor. Mr. Peters carried Buster upstairs and settled him on the couch. Katie teased Buster about getting the whole household quarantined, and the little boy looked pleased with himself. Miss Howell helped Mother put hot dogs on the toasting forks, while Miss Julia spread a picnic cloth on the floor, with her jar of relish in the middle. Cousin Ben was getting in her way, telling her all about the time his sister Louisey had diphtheria. Dad put one of his favorite symphony records on the phonograph, and now Mr. Watkins' heavy steps were coming down the stairs, and Mr. Peabody was following him.

Flames tongued orange in the fireplace, drops from

the hot dogs sizzled on the glowing logs, and the old parlor was full of talk as music played softly in the background. Katie John surveyed the scene critically. Everyone was having a good time, everyone was here—everyone but Gladys and Pearl.

She wondered what they were doing. Cooking supper on their hot plate? Washing their stockings and hanging them from the chandelier? Listening to the party down here? Oh, they don't care, she told herself. This isn't their idea of a party, anyway. For party music they'd have that crazy western stuff.

Of course, everyone had his own taste in music . . . it was a little thing, really . . . not as important as being friends . . .

Katie John stared into the fire, the flames almost hypnotizing her. Then she went to Dad and whispered to him. He raised his eyebrows but turned off the phonograph. Katie fiddled with the dials of the radio until she found what she wanted. "I gotta horse that's purtier'n you!" a western singer shouted against the whang of a harmonica. Some of the people looked startled at the burst of noise, but Miss Howell smiled across the room to Katie and gave a little nod, and Mr. Peabody's foot began to tap.

Katie turned the music as loud as she dared and ran upstairs. Pearl answered her knock.

"Listen!" Katie John exclaimed. "The party's lots of fun, and everybody wants you to come down."

Gladys came to the doorway. From below sounded an exciting mixture of fast music, talk, and laughter.

Pearl began to smile. "Why not, Gladys?"

Gladys shrugged and pulled the curlers out of her hair. "Guess we aren't doing anything, anyway. Just to please the kid."

Pearl winked at Katie, and her freckled face didn't look so bad, smiling. "Be right down," she said.

Katie John galloped back down the stairs, two steps at a time. "Gladys and Pearl are coming!" she announced.

Mr. Watkins, who was presiding at the fireplace, put more wieners on the toasting forks. When Gladys and Pearl appeared, he and Mr. Peabody helped them fix hot-dog buns. Soon the two women were laughing and chattering as if they'd planned the party themselves.

Katie John was satisfied. The party was complete. She was just biting into a hot dog that Dad handed her when Cousin Ben called, "Hold on. Whoa, everybody!"

He and Miss Julia had been talking on a settee in a corner. Now he stood up with a big grin in the middle of his whiskers. Miss Julia was smiling down at her hands clasped in her lap.

"Got a little something to tell—well—and this is as good a time as any," Cousin Ben said. "Just want to say—"

For once Ben Orlick seemed to have trouble talking. Katie John stared at him as he pulled helplessly at his beard. And Miss Julia's cheeks were pink. Goodness sakes, what was the matter with them?

"Little lady said 'yes'!" Cousin Ben burst out. "Going to be my wife!"

All Katie could do was stare as everyone exclaimed and pushed around the couple to congratulate them. Gentle Miss Julia and talkety old Cousin Ben? Come to think of it, they did make a pretty good combination. He loved to talk, and she was good at listening. So that's why he'd stayed here so long. He'd been courting Miss Julia. Her prince had come.

"Wow!" Katie cried, jumping up. "A romance right in our house!"

"This calls for a toast," Dad was saying. He poured more apple juice in everyone's glass and lifted his to "the happiest couple in this house!"

"Is Santa Claus gettin' married?" Buster spoke loudly from his place on the couch.

Everyone laughed, and even Cousin Ben chuckled.

"Yes, sir, you little rascal, and I'll see that old Santa remembers you next Christmas."

The fire leaped bright as Christmastime on the cool spring evening, the guitars and harmonicas twanged and whuffled gaily from the radio, and everyone's face shone. Katie John settled on the hearth full of hot dog and popcorn and deep contentment. *Maybe we aren't always one big happy family under this roof. Gladys and Pearl are the same people they always were. But at least we're all one step closer to being friends. And this house is still a home.*

And the Next Day

The next morning Katie John helped her mother clean up the parlor after the party. Mother was trying to scrub mustard stains out of the carpet, while Katie hunted popcorn from under the cushions of the couch and chairs.

"Looks as if people just took handfuls of popcorn and threw them in the air, whoopee," she said, dropping three more kernels in her trash sack. "It was a good party, wasn't it!"

Cousin Ben's surprising announcement had made the party even a happier one than she'd expected. Funny old Cousin Ben. She'd miss him, she realized. But she and her parents would still be seeing him often, for when he and Miss Julia were married next month he'd move to the Howell sisters' farm by the river. He'd said that sister Louisey was too used to running her own house for him to bring a bride home at this stage of life. Next winter Miss Howell would move back to her apartment at the Tuckers' house, but Cousin Ben and Miss Julia would stay on the farm. Miss Julia would manage nicely in the country through the winter with a man on the place, she'd said, blushing.

Mr. Peters knocked on the doorjamb and looked in the open parlor door from the front hall.

"Just wanta thank you folks again," he said. "Helpin' with Buster, and makin' the party."

Buster was feeling fine, he reported, but it would probably be another week before they could move.

He added, "Could maybe bring you a coupla roomers next winter, Miz Tucker. If you want. This is a mighty good place to put up for the winter. Two of my river pals might wanta stay here."

"Why, that's wonderful, Mr. Peters," Mother said. "You drop me a postcard next fall, and I'll save rooms for all of you."

Mr. Peters left, and Katie and Mother were still cleaning when Dad came in from the porch with the mail in his hand. His face was pale.

"Read this," he said, handing a letter to Mother.

Mother glanced at the letter and screamed, "Oh, darling!" throwing her arms around Dad's neck.

"What? What is it?" Katie John ran around them trying to find Mother's hand holding the letter.

She took the sheet and read it quickly.

"Oh! Oh, my goodness!"

An editor wanted to buy Dad's book! Not the first one about the newspaper business, not the one he'd worked on so long, but the second one. The one he'd written in a few months and wouldn't tell what it was about because he said it was just some nonsense.

"Dad! Dad!" Katie pulled at her father's hand. "Now tell us. What's it about?"

Dad grinned. "It's a murder mystery. Set in a rooming house. And a nosy little girl named Annie Pete helps solve the mystery."

"Daddy!" Katie John shrieked. "Did you put me in a book?"

"Certainly not," Dad said, laughing. "Annie Pete is two other girls."

Katie John didn't believe him. She went into giggles of delight and made him promise to let her read his manuscript.

Mother and Dad were planning happily. Now they wouldn't have to worry about money this summer. The advance money that the editor would pay for the book would carry them through. Of course it wasn't a tremendous amount, and they'd continue to rent rooms to the people who were already living in the house. But they wouldn't try to rent to any new people. When the Peters and the Howells and Cousin Ben moved out, they'd let those rooms stand vacant. Katie and Mother wouldn't have to work so hard this summer. Next winter they'd rent the vacant rooms only to Miss Howell and the rivermen.

"The most important thing, though," Mother said, her eyes shining at Dad, "is that your writings will be published."

"Yep." Dad took the letter. "And they want another

book, too. Another mystery with Annie Pete." He winked at Katie John.

Suddenly everything was so wonderful that Katie just had to be off by herself. She hurried out of the house, through Aunt Emily's vegetable garden to the bottom of the yard, and flung herself down on the sunny grass under the old walnut tree. She lay on her stomach until her excitement calmed to a happy hum inside her. When the sun had warmed her hair until it was like a cap, Katie John propped her chin on her hands and looked down into the grass, where an ant was scurrying about.

How nicely everything was working out. Dad's book, Cousin Ben, the renters all friends, more rivermen coming next fall. She'd lived here almost a year now, and all the problems and loose ends were tying up, the way it happened at the end of a book. Now if she were a girl in one of her library books, by this time she'd be all changed and grown up and thankful for some important lesson she'd learned. What had she learned? She thought back over the past year, but it was only a happy blur of gleaming banisters and many sheets on the clotheslines and snowballs and renters' faces bobbing up and a dog with a sniffing nose and a spot at the end of his tail. Of course she'd grown up some. Everybody does in a year's time. But mostly she'd lived a lot.

"Anyway, I'm me," Katie John murmured contentedly, "and I'm going to go right on being me."

The ant was climbing a tall blade of grass now. No

crumb of food in his legs, not working for once, just looking around. The ant reached the top of the blade and stretched his feelers in the sunshine.

Gently Katie John plucked the blade of grass and held it higher.

"Take a good look," she told the ant. "It's a beautiful world."

HARPER TROPHY BOOKS

you will enjoy reading

HARPER & ROW, PUBLISHERS, INC.

10 East 53rd Street, New York, New York 10022